I am a working mother of three beautiful children: Mica, my diamond; Jeremiah, my sunshine; and Josiah, my star. My husband is John, my heart, I love them all so deeply, and without their support this wouldn't be possible. My passion for writing, and different styles of writing, has been with me for the longest time. My other books include *I Am Black* – a personal outlook on life from a perspective of black person; and my children's forever series of books *My Name is Raisin*, - explaining to children that even though we are all different we are the same.

This is a work of fiction. Names, characters, businesses, places, events and incidents are either the products of the author's imagination or used in a fictitious manner. Any resemblance to actual persons, living or dead, or actual events is purely coincidental.

Unspoken *Love*

Trisha Caress

Unspoken *Love*

Vanguard Press

VANGUARD PAPERBACK

© Copyright 2023
Trisha Caress

The right of Trisha Caress to be identified as author of
this work has been asserted by her in accordance with the
Copyright, Designs and Patents Act 1988.

All Rights Reserved

No reproduction, copy or transmission of this publication
may be made without written permission.
No paragraph of this publication may be reproduced,
copied or transmitted save with the written permission of the
publisher, or in accordance with the provisions
of the Copyright Act 1956 (as amended).

Any person who commits any unauthorised act in relation to
this publication may be liable to criminal
prosecution and civil claims for damages.

A CIP catalogue record for this title is
available from the British Library.

ISBN 978 1 80016 523 6

*Vanguard Press is an imprint of
Pegasus Elliot Mackenzie Publishers Ltd.*
www.pegasuspublishers.com

First Published in 2023

**Vanguard Press
Sheraton House Castle Park
Cambridge England**

Printed & Bound in Great Britain

I would like to dedicate this to my forever inspiration, my mother. She knew long before me that I would go forth and do everything I always wanted to do, it has just taken longer than expected. She is no longer with me in body but she will always be beside me in spirit. She was my hero and forever will be.

Also I would like to thank my sister, Michelle. All through our lives we have been close and since our mother passed we are even closer. We live in different towns but are constantly in touch, every morning and evening. She makes sure I focus and is so proud of all I have achieved and going to achieve. Thank you, sis, I will love and cherish you always, Tx

Thank you to all the people in my life who have doubted and believed in me; both parties have pushed me equally to be stronger and to be the best version of myself, and for that I love you all. Hiya, see ya, bye Tx

Chapter *One*

The first time I saw him was at the swimming pool. I had been here for half an hour. I was in the water just taking a few minutes break, as I was out of breath and out of shape. My stomach was wobbly, my thighs were too big my body just wasn't how I wanted it to be, only I could change this. So there I was resting at the side of the pool, no makeup, and my hair was dripping wet, and out of the corner of my eye, there he was, walking towards the pool. His perfectly toned body, his thick thighs made me gasp. I read every ripple on his torso. He turned around ready to dive into the pool, oh my. *Oh my*! His bottom and his manhood held by those tights blue shorts... I wished it was the palms of my hands. He dived into the pool, the water dividing like waves in the ocean. This beautiful being, tanned from top to bottom, mmm, mmm. I had to pull myself together, as I needed to do a few more laps. I only managed one as I could no longer concentrate.

I got out of the pool, draped my towel around me, very quickly. Just one more quick glance, he swam like a merman, he was absolutely beautiful, chiselled jaw, perfect chin, perfect cheek bones, brown greenish eyes, lips that my lips wanted to meet – would he ever notice me? I don't even notice me. I am just your average girl next door, nothing to write home about. I am working on it, I will turn heads, yes I will, I have been telling myself this for a few years, only I can change me.

My name is Essence.

Chapter Two

The next day, it dawned on me. It was a sunny Sunday, my head thick from the alcohol last night. As I fell onto the sofa, the grey throw just seemed to wrap around me, like it knew I needed the comfort. I sipped on my fresh lemon tea; the steam engulfed my nostrils. A piece of toast was all I could stomach. Me and my throw felt like we were one at that moment, so I didn't want to move from that very spot, but I had a word with myself, which I very often did.

I get up, carry myself up the stairs. I enter my closet, and rifle through my endless amount of clothes, which are in numerous sizes that I will fit into at some point. I pick out ten outfits, maybe more, take them to my bedroom, and I derobe as I am so hot and so very sweaty. I must have a shower, I head to the bathroom. I pick my favourite scent, Sensuous, bypass the shower and fill my bath with bubbles. They float on top of the water with some escaping into the air, flower petals surrounding the bathroom, the steam of the water moving around the room popping the bubbles that escaped.

I dip my toe in with an ooo, I turn on the cold tap to take away some of the heat, candles lit, the wax melts down the sides, a swift scent of jasmine, I inhale and let a deep breath out. My robe slips from my moist body lying onto the glittering tiles of my bathroom floor. I put my right leg into the bubbles, my left leg follows. I gently ease my body into the fragrant water, bubbles surrounding me. I feel my skin touching the porcelain of the bath. Romantic music plays bouncing from each wall, just loud enough to surround my ears. It's Luther Vandross, his voice as smooth as a rose petal. I close my eyes and rest onto the bath pillow, which cradles my head. I drift asleep, and I feel his hand.

My thoughts run wild; I feel his hands sweeping my body. His fingers sweep my lips. I kiss them slowly until one enters my mouth. He then caresses and kisses the nape of my neck and flows down to my breasts, his firm lips and tongue flickering across my nipples. With a deep sigh his hands are around my waist, squeezing, and touching my hips. Pulling me gently towards him, he put his hands between my thighs, moving his beautiful big hands to and fro until swiftly moving to my silk, he has created, he penetrates me with his fingers over and over again. My body can't take it anymore, I have to let go. I bite my lip as I orgasm; the pleasure I feel is mind blowing. I let out a scream as he takes his hands away.

Then I realise it was me doing all these things to myself, I was only dreaming it was him. I woke, lifted myself out of the bath, droplets of water fall from my body. I pat myself down with a towel, thereafter, adding just enough baby oil to my body, every inch of my skin is now aglow. My bathrobe now adorns my body and I think I will lay on the bed, still so tired from the night before, just an hour or two snooze.

Chapter *Three*

I feel well rested, had a bit more sleep than expected, but obviously needed. A deep breath out and a stretch off, I sit up, taking a look at all the dresses I got out earlier. Do I wear floaty, clingy, long or short? Who am I kidding? Of course it's a floaty number; my body wasn't ready for the others yet. The dress I decide to wear is green and shows just a little cleavage, and the bottoms of my legs. I sit in front of my dresser, makeup lights on, apply just a little makeup. My father always told me I was a natural beauty, but then again he is my father. A brush of my curly hair and a sweep of lipstick, and I step into my floaty dress. I slip into my three inch court shoes and that is it.

Just as I was about to grab my bag my best friend arrives. In she walks looking fierce, absolutely stunning. A very short orange dress adorned her body, heels as high as six inches. I felt like a frump looking at her, and although she had those heels on I was still taller. Five foot eleven, and I still don't get noticed; if it's a nerdy-geeky guy I might get a look in.

Off we went to the wine bar. As we walked in all eyes were on us, again who am I kidding? They were all on my friend, I can dream, can't I? I feel like a spare part.

"Let's get some drinks, a large glass of wine for me and a cocktail for my bestie." The barman told us someone had paid for the cocktail, but not the wine. How rude!

I was used to it. I told Aurora, and yes her name is as beautiful as she is, that it can't be a late night as I'm at work tomorrow. I am a legal secretary, so I need to keep a clear head. All through the evening Aurora was inundated with compliments. I ended up talking to the 'friend' and it's always the one with the bad breath. I think I puked in my mouth at one point from the stench. I had to move, she must have had ten phone numbers in her bag, and they're all ending up in the bin at the end of the night. She got a few kisses and enjoyed the drinks that were bought for her; she only went into her bag once and that was to buy me that large glass of wine.

"Aurora, I'm going home," I told her.

She gave me a hug and I left. Obviously, she was going to stay; she didn't have a job, and her daddy was rich. I wasn't mad at her; we have been friends since we were in infant school. We are twenty-five now. She had long flowing red hair, blue eyes and a figure I could only dream of. I will get there.

I am home now, time to clean off my makeup and sort my suit out for the morning.

Ah, my bed feels like heaven, its ten thirty. I'm not going to put my TV on, or music. I am going to try and go straight to sleep. Or not.

Tick tock, tick tock. Eleven, twelve, one and two and I'm still wide awake. Why can I not sleep? Yawn, I am so knackered, maybe I shouldn't have had those few hours earlier. Around four I must have dozed off. My alarm was set for half past six. I'm going to need match sticks for these eyes today.

Chapter *Four*

I scrape myself out of bed, literally. Gym clothes on and off I go, so glad I have my little Mini outside, as today I will not be walking. I arrive at the gym, so daunting, but I must push myself. Treadmill, half an hour I say to myself, but fifteen minutes is all I can manage, so I sit on the exercise bike for fifteen minutes going at a slow pace. Then I go lift a few weights and also do some floor exercises. It's time to leave. I walk past a huge mirror and tell myself, you must do better, Essence, you will get to that size that you want. A quick shower and now it's time for work.

We have a very big case. Being a legal secretary is no mean feat. Sometimes we have to work long hours, writing legal letters, documents and Wills. I have my legal secretary diploma so I have excellent administration skills and IT skills. At the moment I only work three days a week, but they are twelve hour days. My boss, Michael, is a lot older but easy on the eye. He and his personal assistant, Amanda, are at it like rabbits. I found used condoms in the bin a few weeks back and then the other day I knocked at Michael's office door and I could of swore he said come in, so I opened the door and there they were, her lying on the table and him with his trousers around his ankles. They were going at it, neither of them noticed that I was there, so I stepped back out of the door while watching them. I couldn't actually believe what I was seeing.

The phone was ringing at my desk, he must have heard, because there was a lot of banging and the sound of things falling to floor. It was one of his colleagues; I put the phone call through. Amanda came scuttling out, bleach blonde hair, made up like she was on a night out, a gold digger if ever there was one. She has a name around the offices, the bike.

It's a big firm. My boss Michael is not the top man around here, he is the fourth one down and Amanda, has and will sleep with whoever she has to, to get wherever she wants. I don't think I have seen her do any work, she was just a gofer when she started.

There are over a hundred people working in this building. It's a den of iniquity, you could write a book about all the shenanigans. We have a guy called Kevin who snorts cocaine in the toilets. Most of us know about it, he works much better on that stuff. It's also a case of when he doesn't have it he doesn't have an ounce of personality. There's another secretary and my other best friend, her name's Lucy, She has had everything on her body enhanced, her lips, bottom, even her hips. She can barely sit down. She is so funny, a great person to talk to and the stories she comes out with are just unimaginable. She is also a lap dancer; she told me on her shift last night that a punter she had threw loads of money at her. "Please!" he pleaded, "make my penis erect, my girlfriend keeps laughing at me saying that I can't even get it up."

So Lucy, who's really professional at what she does, turned round and said, "Okay, sir, I will do my best." She danced around, gyrated on his lap with nothing but a G-string on. He loved every minute of it, grunted like a pig. He was a really big guy, sweating and panting. "Yes! Yes!" he said. "You have made me get an erection. Look, look!" he said as he pulled his trousers down and then his Y-fronts. Lucy said to me she nearly fell off her heels – his penis was as small as a mushroom. It was actually smaller than his balls. Inside she was laughing so hard.

He was so pleased. "Do you think my girlfriend will enjoy me now?"

Forever the professional she is, she said, "Of course." She picked up all the money and off she went to her dressing room. She laughed so hard at the mushroom man, which she will call him from now on. "He was just so adorable and just couldn't understand why he couldn't satisfy his girlfriend."

I need to get back to doing my work, I look at the time, it was seven-thirty. Scratch that, time to go home. I will finish off tomorrow.

Back home, I decide to go for a walk to clear my head.

Chapter *Five*

The sun is still shining, although it's gone past eight; these long summer nights are so much appreciated. I put on a blue flowery off the shoulder dress, just above the knee, and some sparkly sandals with my sunnies and off I go.

Nothing could have prepared me. I could never have expected the man I desire in front of me, the man, from the pool, from my dreams. I watched him walking towards me; it felt like it was in slow motion, the breeze blowing, his brown greenish eyes piercing mine. I look away as every bone in my body feels like it's shaking. Am I walking all right? I find myself pulling my shoulders back, bust out. Thank heavens I wore a dress.

I raise my eyes, he was gone. He had already walked past me. My face reddened, beads of sweat on my top lip, how embarrassing. Next time I will be ready and pluck up the courage to say hello. I have dreamt about him so many, no too many times. Only in my wildest dreams he is mine. Now I know he walks this way I will be walking frequently; I sound like a stalker, ha-ha. I laugh at myself as it just dawned on me, he wasn't giving me eye contact because I had sunnies on, what an idiot ha-ha.

I get back home and the phone's ringing. Yes, I still have a home phone. It was my boyfriend. I failed to mention I was in a relationship, a year and half it's been dragging along. We've never lived together, in fact we do not do much of anything together. I thought I loved him, but I know now I simply don't, he's just there. How could I love someone if my mind is full of a man with no name? I feel as if I'm caught in a storm. It feels as if he is raining down on me, and I don't want him to stop, the wind is pulling me from side to side, whirlwind is carrying me, the sun is always shining. A rainbow appears, that's how the man with no name makes me feel.

Calvin was on a different level, that's my boyfriend's name. Calvin was a routine man. He is five years older than me. We would see each other two times a week; one would be at his house and one may be at the cinema or bowling. Sex was me laid down, him on top. I starting faking orgasms after the first month but felt for some reason, he will do, so I've just been getting on with it.

You see my parents separated when I was about five. I lived with my dad until I got my own place at twenty years old. That's perhaps why I'm still with Calvin, for stability. I didn't want to be like my mother, she had an affair for years before Dad found out. She was a nurse.. I was an only child. Mum went on to have two more children, and I have never met them as I will not see her. My dad did everything possible to make sure I had a good life. We would go on holiday twice a year, not abroad, but on holiday still. Cornwall was Dads favourite as he loves fishing. We stayed in caravans and/or lodges. Dad taught me how to read and write, how to swim, we went everywhere together. He didn't have friends around or go to the pubs, he would drink at home but only a beer or two at the weekends. He loved gardening, I would go outside with him and he showed me how to grow vegetables, and plant flowers. When my friends from school had birthday parties at their home he would take me and sit in his car and wait no matter how long I was. You see he never wanted me to come to harm, some may say overprotective but that didn't bother me as I knew no different.

As I got older we had to go shopping for underwear. I was turning into a woman. My dad was a little embarrassed buying my bras, nothing sexy, just T-shirt bras. In turn I was embarrassed when my periods started, even though we were taught at school. I didn't know how to approach my dad to get me some sanitary wear, so for the first two months of my cycle I used toilet paper, as I was only on light, and they would last only four days, but the toilet paper would make me sore, so in the end I braved it and just blurted it out that I had got my period. I should have known better; he had already brought me some sanitary wear and some white sanitary bags and left them in the bathroom drawer, the one I hardly went in. My dad is the best, my dad, Claud.

Chapter *Six*

My stomach is rumbling. Bloody hell, I haven't eaten at all day today, I wondered why I felt a little lightheaded. Let's see what's in the fridge. Mm pork chops, my favourite. I will do them with lots of veg, no carbs for a while, need to lose some of this body fat. My dad taught me how to cook. You will hear me refer to him a lot, sorry not sorry, ha-ha. Let me cut up some onions, pork chops in the pan first and brown each side, add onions, some all-purpose seasoning and garlic granules, add a bit more vegetable oil, cook to perfection, pot of veg on. How the hell am I going to eat all of this?

I did while watching catch up TV. I am still hungry, nope, no more food, pint of water, a quick shower and then to bed, gym early again. Night, night.

Chapter *Seven*

The alarm goes off, feels like I have only been asleep for a minute. I do not want to get up today so I snooze the alarm another eight or nine minutes, shut my eyes and off goes the alarm again, dare I snooze it again? No, Essence, get up, I say to myself. I drag my gym gear on, brush my teeth, wash the sleep out of my eyes and off I go. I love my little car. Dad bought it me. I hate the colour though, lime green, but it's mine and as I said my dad bought it for me. It's really quiet on the road at this early hour.

I get to the gym. My eyes must be deceiving me – there he was, right in front of me, the man with no name. He was walking up the stairs. I couldn't tear my eyes away from these big thick thighs, his bottom clenching as he walks. I suddenly felt flushed; I was giddy with excitement. He was right there as I approached the reception desk to sign in. He glances back; I put my eyes towards the floor.

The lady behind the desk said, "Excuse me, miss, do you want to sign in?" I was frozen to the floor, for a second or two. "Excuse me, miss," she said again.

"Erm, yes," I said. I went to the locker, wait I don't need a locker. My eyes skirted around the gym to see where he was, and I clocked him on the treadmill. There was one behind him on the other side. I put in ten minutes incline. He was running on his, I was walking, well I think I was, I was all in a daze.

I watched every inch of his body move; his calves so tight and prominent, his thighs, oh my, those thighs, I wish they were wrapped around me. His bottom was so plump. My eyes moved up to his waist, everything went in slow motion. I bit my lip with wanting in my groin. His back was pulsating out of his tight T-shirt, his neck just the right thickness… if only I could press my lips slowly all over it. His hair dark and perfectly coiffed. My admiration of this perfect man soon came to an abrupt end as my ten minutes had finished, did I even do any walking?

If nothing else I was walking on air. I put another ten minutes on as he was still going, I will only move when he does, another twenty minutes pass, I simply couldn't do anymore, so I take my time, wipe the handles, then precede to take a long sip of my water, he started to walk slowly, must be on his cool down, not long now Yes, I cheer to myself he has finished. I watch him walk to the floor weights, he went to one of the benches nearby. Stomach in, I walked towards him, I mean, the weights. I lay on the floor and start with some stomach crunches. I did about six, who was I kidding? I couldn't do them, my stomach was cramping up, so I got on all fours, now holding some small weights, pretending I knew what I was doing. Right leg pushed out, then up, then left leg, repeat, I stood up with these little weights, arms straight out to the sides while crooking my neck, watching my dream man with no name.

He looked over, so, me with a shy smile, whispered, "Hi."

To my astonishment he answered back, "Hello," with a deep manly voice I nearly dropped my weights.

What do I say now? I was all a flutter. So I said nothing, I put the weights down, gave him a smile and walked off to my car. Oh bloody hell, I've left my towel. Oh well I said to myself, he said hello. Oh my, he said hello.

I am going to be late for work so I must get a move on; I have seven days off after this, so I will persevere today. As I walked in, Michael was on the prowl. Something has pissed him off.

"Where the bloody hell have you been? You're late!" he shouted.

"Sorry, Michael, it was traffic."

"Leave earlier! Now get to flaming work, you have all of Mr. Blacks papers to type up and email over !"

It slipped out my mouth. "Where's Amanda? She's your PA she should be doing that not me."

"What did you say?" Michael shouted.

"Erm, Erm nothing!" I just did what he asked, Amanda wasn't in, she gets away with everything as being his mistress, we've all seen all the lavish gifts she's been given. "Cow!" I said under my breath. I cannot wait to move up in the ranks, the firm is called Legal Eagles; I have never met the number one boss.

This day is going to be long. I had eleven hours in front of me, and I'm knackered, but right now none of that matters because he said hello, the man with no name said hello!

Well, my day just got worse; Michael has sent Joyful to help with Amanda's workload that she hasn't finished. How Joyful got that name is beyond me, she is anything but. She has made so many enemies with her lies and deceit; she tries to get in everyone's business and twist things to her own version. Her tongue is venomous. At first people would believe what she was saying, as she plays that game so well.

I was sitting in a cubicle a while back, she didn't know I was there. Mavis and she were having a chit chat, Mavis didn't like her but Joyful was near her pension age so she appeased her. She told Mavis that she heard Lucy was a prostitute and that she can be found on the streets at night. She then went on to tell her that Lucy was sexually assaulted in a layby which was completely untrue. I was listening with complete disgust.

Then she spoke of Kevin, how he was a druggy and how Lucy and he were sleeping together, and of course he was paying her to do so. I couldn't listen any more so I came out of the toilet. She was shocked to see me. I looked at her and my eyes scalded that bitch. I washed my hands and walked out.

Mavis followed very swiftly. "I didn't believe a word of it, Essence!"

"So why did you stand and say nothing? Why were you so comfortable to listen to that crap from that evil bitch?"

Of course I got no reply, she just went red in the face.

I obviously told Lucy, she was absolutely mortified and so angry, but I told her not to give her any satisfaction in arguing with her, as her time would come. Joyful is only here for another month then she's gone.

Anyway, sitting here with her I couldn't wait for a break, so I've text Lucy and asked her to meet for lunch.

Back to typing out these papers, my eyes burned with how much I have typed out. I do have to give myself credit as I did everything Michael asked me to do, and I also finished the rest of the work that I left last night.

Lunch time fast approached. Lucy and I went for lunch at the restaurant across the way.

"I really need a drink."

"So do I! Let's just not mention it when we get back!" she laughed, so we had a large white wine and ordered our food.

"So, Lucy, about Joyful, what shall we do about her?"

"I have an idea, but tell me what do you think first?" Lucy said. "Well I would like to find a big cauldron, boil some water, put some salt and pepper in it and put her in!" We laughed hard at that as we knew that kind of thing is not viable or legal.

"-Or how about we put pee in her tea? Or make her a face mask with dog shit ? Ha-ha!"

"No, Lucy, that's so mean. I do have idea though and something that we could actually do."

"Let's order another wine first," Lucy said excitedly, waiting to hear my idea.

"Well Joyful retires in four weeks so let's plan her a leaving do, in the big empty office upstairs, the one with the bar we use for our Christmas party. We will invite everyone, to wish her well, but no one will be there, she will just have a screen of everyone leaving what messages they desire. We will use the old decorations, put a few nibbles on, and play a playlist on a little Bluetooth speaker. We have to swear all to secrecy. The only one we can't tell is Kevin as he cannot keep it to himself when he has a sniff or rub of the gum with the white stuff!"

Lucy looked at me with bright eyes. "Sounds like a plan to me!"

We chatted some more and laughed our way through lunch before we headed back to work with a spring in our step. As I sat down, though, I was contemplating if we should go ahead with the plan to get back at Joyful. She's just a bitter old lady; her only social life is work. Could that be why she makes shit up, and hurts people's feelings with that vile mouth of hers? Wouldn't we be just as bad as her?

I started my filing, somehow it had all changed and things weren't where they should be, or should I say where i like them to be, so I need to put it back to my system so it's easier for me, I hate it when people don't put things back where they came from. This last hour is dragging, but at this moment I am so glad it did, Amanda has just arrived.

"Hey!" I said. She just looked at me. My eyes glanced at her tummy, oh my, she looks pregnant. Come to think of it, some of the girls have heard her puking in the toilets, and her and Michael have been at it like God knows what in his office. I had thought nothing of it but now I know why he wasn't in the best of moods this morning.

She closed his office door behind her, but she may as well have left it open, the arguing was so loud.

I called Lucy, she then called Mavis and some of the other girls followed. "Lucy!" I said, "For God's sake, I only called you!"

Amanda was demanding Michael to leave his wife. Of course, he said no. "Well I will tell her every fucking thing."

"I gave you no promises!" Michael replied.

"Yes you did! I am carrying your child for fuck's sake. I live in a poky little apartment with one room, how am I supposed to give my, no, our child—"

"Get rid of the baby," he said.

"I can't and I won't, I am five and half months gone!"

Michael answered, "And how do I know the baby's mine?"

"Are you fucking kidding me?!" she shouted. "Of course it's yours and I am keeping it!"

"Well I want a DNA test" he said.

Amanda screamed, "You absolute bastard, I fucking hate you!" We could hear and see her scrambling to the door.

All the girls tried to run to their desks. I just pretended I was looking through paperwork. "Bye!" I said.

"Oh fuck off!" she said to me and off she went, so angry steam was coming out of her ears.

Michael called me into the office. "Essence, go home and tell Joyful to go too."

"Okay, are you sure Michael?"

"Yes! Just go home!"

"I will see you in eight days then. As I am on annual leave."

"Essence, enjoy your time off," he said.

"Okay. See you when I get back, call me if you should need me." Shit why did I say that? Why the hell did say that? I am going to spoil myself with shopping, pamper days, nights out and the gym, swimming and spending quality time with my dad, so I hope Michael doesn't even think about calling me.

Chapter *Eight*

*T*onight I am going out with Aurora and Lucy. These two are so glamorous, how would I compare? What shall I wear?

I decided on my tight fitting, red, bust popping dress. I shaved every part of my body that had a hint of hair, armpits, legs, top lip and my private area, you never know ha-ha. I haven't had sex for a while. Calvin and I don't even see each other much now, I really need to be honest with him, he doesn't even cross my mind. Did I actually love him? Was it lust? Not really, or did I just want a companion? Maybe I did love him but never in love. Since I have seen the man with no name he's I all I can think about and now that he has spoken to me, well, I say spoken, he said hello, it's a start.

I will handle telling Calvin how I feel with care. I cannot take away what a kind and gentle man he is and I truly do not want to hurt him but it's hurting me to stay.

Oh my, I need to get ready, the girls will be here soon, shower and shave done, now my makeup. Red lips tonight. I straighten out my hair and slip my red dress on. It's a bit tight but luckily it's a stretchy material. The underwear I am wearing pulls me in and lifts up my breasts. I had to release the straps though as they almost touched my chin, and I laughed out loud. I could almost kiss them. Let me just put some oil on my legs, no one wants to see ashy skin. This dress requires four inch heels, gosh my feet are going to die tonight. Right, now, time for the checks: money, yes, lipstick, yes, brush, yes, chewing gum, yes. right on time the girls arrive.

Off we go. First we stop at a wine bar. "What are we having tonight?"

I spot a cocktail menu. "I think I'm going to have cocktail, hmm let's see...oo this sounds nice, I'm going to have a Trish delish!"

Aurora has a Special G, Lucy has a wine. I have never heard of these cocktails before but they have more alcohol than juice, may as well start the night as we mean to go on. Aurora is being chatted up already. So glad Lucy is with us. She wasn't her normal self-tonight, though.

"What's the matter Luc?"

"Essence, a month back I slept with one of my clients."

"What?" I asked, "You said you would never do that, you only tease these people, what on earth were you thinking?"

"Well, that's it, I wasn't thinking. I have slept with him more than once. My job is to turn people on, but this guy did that exact thing for me!"

"So what's the problem?" I ask confused.

"Well first of all we didn't use protection. I have no excuse really as the first time there was a few of us drinking and laughing and then we were the only ones left in the strip club and as it was a very quiet night, the boss left me with the keys. I locked the doors, and just me and this guy were left. I love my job but I am a human being, I have feelings too. I needed to have sex with him, a man – my toys and me were getting tedious – to feel flesh inside me to feel his movements against mine, to kiss his mouth, Essence," Lucy explained.

"Okay I get it, so are you going to tell me what's troubling you then? You're not pregnant are you?"

"No! That's the least of my problems, I have been feeling really unwell lately. Can we go sit somewhere quieter?"

"Okay! Let's go over there, I will get us some drinks first." Lucy sat waiting patiently for me. "Right, Lucy just spit it out!"

"Okay! Okay! I have been itching down there, and I thought it was thrush from all the toys, so I got the required stuff but nothing happened. Now everything is swollen and sore, little Luce, as I call her, isn't little right now."

"You mean your vagina? What do you think it is? Are you getting a smelly discharge as well?" I asked.

"Yes and boy does it smell. One of my other clients complained to my boss that I smelt fishy, I was so embarrassed," Lucy replied, red faced.

"Have you been to the doctor yet?"

"No I haven't! How can I face my family doctor?"

"Well how long have you had these symptoms?" I quizzed, sounding like a doctor myself.

"About three and a half weeks!"

"You need to go to the doctors, for crying out loud. Are you stupid? This kind of thing can take over your whole body, especially if it's something serious. It's probably something easily treated. Get a grip. I will come with you, make the appointment in the morning."

"Sorry if I have put a downer on your evening."

"Come on, the evening has just begun let's put all our troubles aside and enjoy the rest of it," I said, giving her a reassuring smile.

Aurora came over.

"What are you two gossiping about?" she asked.

"More importantly, what have you been doing? Or should I say who?" I interjected before she could ask anything else. Phew, that put her off the scent.

"Well, the guy who's been chatting me up is about forty-five, absolutely loaded and wants to take me out later tonight. I think he said is name is Pete, do you mind?"

"Well as a matter of fact, Aurora, I do! What if Lucy wasn't here? We are meant to be on a girls' night out!" I had to tell her,

"Essy, don't be like that, you know what I am like!" she said.

"Yes I bloody well do and I am sick of feeling used by you. I no longer want to be your prop for meeting guys when you are out. For once can't you put your best friend first? Can't you see that it pisses me off?" I snapped.

"Sounds like you're jealous to me! Essy, I am going regardless! He could be the one! And I said he is loaded! Bye!"

Cheeky bitch, I thought as she walked away. I can't believe it.

Lucy and I moved onto a nightclub. We went straight to the toilet to freshen up. The night was doomed, I thought, Lucy with all her problems, Rora leaving like that. I look at myself in the mirror and say, "I didn't squeeze into this dress for nothing, let's do this." We danced and we consumed quite a few cocktails. We decided to go into the next room, a singles room. We had to pay a bit more to go into it but got a large glass of champagne on entrance.

As we scoped the room I thought, look at the state of some of these men and they wonder why they are single, dressed in dirty ripped clothes, and I've seen a few people with hardly any teeth. Just unkempt, how did they even get in here? Some of the women are just as bad.

"Let's get out of here." I said, I couldn't stand it anymore.

Lucy clearly wasn't in the mood either with all that's going on and drinking isn't going to solve anything for us. We went back to into the other room and although we said we were going home we decided to have one more drink.

"Essence, are you going to tell Calvin then? You clearly do not love him," Lucy asked.

"Yes, I do, I'm just not in love with him! It's just how I am going to tell him anyway, never mind about me, what about you? Are you going to make an appointment? If not at the doctors, the STI clinic but at least at the doctors it's just you and he or she. Can you imagine if you go to the STI clinic and you see people in the waiting room? It's obvious what you are there for," I said.

"We are all there for the same reason, I will sort it," she said, squirming in her chair. "I will let you know when I plan on going, Will you come with me?"

"Of course, I told you before that I would, just make the appointment. Let's finish our drinks and go."

As we were walking out of the door Aurora was walking towards us with the older fella, Pete, I think she said his name was.

"Hey girlies!" she said.

I just looked at her, Lucy said whatever and we just carried on to the taxi rank. I was so vexed with her. She is my best friend and I'm meant to be hers but I will not let her continue to use me like this. We have been best friends for years and it's always been this way. Aurora is absolutely beautiful, stunning, her red hair has always made her centre of attention. It really didn't bother me when we were growing up as if it wasn't for her I wouldn't have had so many friends. She attracted everyone's attention, good or bad, mainly good though.

Some girls would be envious and would have a go at her but I would always protect her from them. That's where my weight and stature would come in. I was always the tallest and biggest; no one would pick on me or my bestie.

Through our latter teenage years, that's when the boys came in. She loved all the attention. She would leave me in night clubs, bars, anywhere really to go off with these men.

Well, now it's come to that point I will no longer sit back and be treated this way. She needs to know that I am worthy, so from this night I will not be going out with Aurora on my own. Of course I want to remain best friends but I need to be respected, by everyone around me. I will be telling her tomorrow.

The taxi drops Lucy off first. "Call me," I shouted out of the window, then off I went.

As I arrived home, door locked and chained, I put the kettle on and made myself a hot chocolate, sat on my sofa and thought, what a crap night, it's time I got my life in order. I need to go to bed. Tomorrow is a new day.

In and out of sleep all night, I feel so tired this morning. A cold shower to wake me up, doesn't really work, at least I am refreshed.

The phone rings it's Lucy, telling me she had the appointment at the STI clinic – she couldn't get in the doctors – it's in half an hour. She asked me again, "Can you make it?"

"Of course, I was waiting for your call to be honest. Let me chuck some clothes on and I will pick you up, see you in a shorty."

Lucy was extremely nervous the whole way to the STI clinic, but I put some music on for our short journey to calm her nerves. We arrived and I parked the car. We got into the waiting room and who should we see there, only bloody Joyful, with a young lad.

"Hello!" I said. Oh fuck's sake, the whole workplace will know when she gets back that we were there.

"Lucy Brand." Her name was called but we were deep in conversation about Joyful and what a spiteful bitch she is.

"Old bag!" Lucy said, we laughed as we were looking at her. She knew we were talking about her.

"Lucy Brand," the nurse called again. We got up to go in.

"She's my friend, I want her to come in with me," Lucy told the nurse.

"What seems to be the problem?" the doctor asked.

"Well, I, er, er…"

"Don't worry I am not here to judge, I am here to help you. Now let's start again, what's your symptoms?"

Lucy explained that she's been getting discharge, and a burning sensation, also a fishy smell.

"Are you itching as well, Lucy?"

"Yes."

"Sounds like you may have contracted trichomoniasis. Can you get on the bed in the next room? So we can see what we can do."

Lucy looked terrified as she took off her trousers and underwear, but I was right there with her.

"I'm just going to take a couple of swabs, this might a feel a little uncomfortable." The doctor continued.

She was holding my hand, you could see how nervous she was.

"Right I'm going to look at these under the microscope and I'll be back," the doctor said as he left the room.

"See, that wasn't too bad was it?" I asked Lucy.

"I suppose not, now I just want to get out of here!" she replied whilst getting herself together. After roughly about ten minutes the doctor came back.

"I was right, you have got trichomoniasis. I am going to prescribe you some antibiotics. Do not engage in sex until the infection has cleared up and when you do, do it safely, as next time it could be much worse," he said as he walked over to his desk.

"Thank you so much, Doctor." Lucy was so relieved. "Why didn't I go when I first noticed?" she said, ashamed and embarrassed. She told me that she even thought about giving up her second job.

I asked, "Why would you? It's not your fault, the client you had sex with should have known he had something wrong with his winky!"

She laughed.

"All jokes aside though, Luc, you have been really foolish, sleeping with your client. This is not a film and you're not Julia Roberts, ha-ha."

We fell into the car laughing.

"I'm just glad it's sorted now and trust me, I won't be sleeping with anyone without protection. I have learnt my lesson. Do you want to go for a drink?"

"No, Lucy I have a few things to sort of my own, but I'll call you later. I will drop you off at the chemist." As I got home my thoughts turned to Calvin.

Chapter *Nine*

I have been so concerned about telling him, but we have seemingly come to an end in our relationship, I just don't want to hurt him. I feel no remorse in what I was going to say, but never the less he would be devastated. We have been together for a year and a half. What if he asked me why? Would I be able to be brutally honest and tell him the truth? That in the bedroom it was boring as hell, with him lasting only five minutes, and that I faked orgasms. He did have a nice size penis, but it served no purpose to me. Our lives together were routine, week after week. He wouldn't be adventurous with food either: bangers and mash, pie and chips, burger and chips. Everything had to have tomato ketchup on it. Rice, pasta or anything else was alien to him. He wore old fashioned clothes too, corduroys, plaid shirts, and don't get me started on the shoes, and Y-fronts. There was nothing trendy or exciting about him; he has only just started wearing aftershave. He made absolutely no effort in anything he did. He worked with computers, there was not a thing he didn't know about them. He would play on his PlayStation every night, even when I was there with him; he was a technophile.

Our way of life were completely opposite. I love the glam look, loved all kinds of food and loved meeting people.

I should be meeting him in a few hours but think I will give it a miss.

I've just called him and made up some excuse that I had a headache and will call him tomorrow.

He said, "That's fine, I have work to do anyway."

I thought that was a bit cold, he didn't even say love you, as he always does. I brushed it off and went to bed for a few hours; working all these long hours, going to the gym etc, was wearing me out. As soon as my head hit that pillow, I was out cold.

The man with no name appeared in my dreams. "Let's dance," he said.

"What right here? Look at all these people!"

"So what?" he said.

"Let's go over there, there aren't so many people," I suggested.

"No, right here," he replied.

"Erm, okay," I said nervously. My AirPods were in and I was listening to George Benson, my dad's favourite. I loved it too as it's all I heard growing up, the classics, so I gave him the left one. He swept me into his arms. I felt as light as a beautiful butterfly, my feet didn't feel the floor. He pulled me in, his hands on my waist, now into the nape of my back. I could feel every finger caress my skin. I felt intoxicated. He put his right leg in between mine, his lips cushioned mine. I felt a sweep of his tongue; he kissed me passionately, my mouth couldn't hold the moisture. He drew me in even closer and I could feel his penis, hard, rubbing against me.

I had no control. silk escaped the side of my G-string. I could feel it trickle down my thigh. His hands were all over me. He discreetly put his hand between my legs and felt my silk. He let out a moan and put his fingers in his mouth.

"Mmm, you taste so good."

I grinded on his manhood so hard I thought I was going to orgasm there and then.

I kept hearing a knocking sound. Stirring. No, I cannot wake from this dream. Another loud knock, I jolted from my dream and sleep. I was so mad it took me a few minutes to compose myself. Another knock. I wasn't expecting anyone.

I got to the door, pizza delivery for next bloody door. Boy, was I pissed but since I had been disturbed and was up I decided to go for a walk, it was a bit chilly, just how I like it. I fancied a hot chocolate, so a stop off at Choc Chips the coffee shop not too far from me, the best hot chocolate place around.

I sit in a window seat. Ordered my drink and a donut, yes, I know I'm meant to be eating well. My drink and sweet arrived. I take a sip of my hot chocolate and a bite of my donut and a deep sigh and reminisce about my dream. As I peered longingly out of the window, whom should I see Calvin! Calvin? Across the way at the bus stop with a woman. He was holding her hand. She leaned in for a kiss and he kissed her right back. I had to rub my eyes and look again. Yes it was him! With another woman! What! Rain started falling against the windowpane. I took another glance but the bus must have come and gone as they were no longer there.

My mind was having a conversation. Did I just see Calvin with another woman? Did my eyes deceive me? I must be having another dream, no way could Calvin do this to me, he is Mr. Bland. Mr. Routine. When I actually look back at the last few months when he started wearing aftershave, and it wasn't old spice. His shirts were also a bit tighter fitting. I thought nothing of it I just thought he wanted to smell good and probably put on a couple of pounds, I stopped looking at him in that way. How blind could I have been?

I am not going to believe it, not until I have a talk with him. I couldn't finish my hot chocolate and donut as I was in disbelief. I am going to make my way home. As I step out of Choc Chip it was still raining. I crossed over the road and sat in the bus stop to see if when I was looking over I wasn't seeing things. I could see clearly into that shop, so my eyes weren't deceiving me.

I carried on home. Door locked and chained behind me, I know, let me call him on his mobile to let him know my headache is much better and that I needed to chat. Of course he didn't answer.

I plonked myself on the sofa with a glass of wine, next thing I knew I had drunk the whole bottle. I open another. Bloody hell, I said to myself, if Calvin doesn't want me who will? I probably have no chance with the man with no name.

I wonder how long has he been seeing that woman? What has she got that I haven't? Where did they meet? Does he work with her? I was really hurt, mostly because he did that to me! He has another woman. I won't know the answers until I see him. I fell asleep on the sofa, wined out.

Chapter *Ten*

An opened full bottle of wine accompanied by an empty one, whoa, my head is banging. Let me look at the time it is, half eight in the morning, that wine knocked me out.

Right, so I am on it today., not the best start though, I've had an argument with my best friend, Lucy. She's worried about having an STI. Right now that is the least of my worries, my boyfriend is seeing some other women I pluck up the courage to call him.

"Hey, Calvin, sorry about last night, I tried to call you to tell you my headache had abetted, but you didn't answer."

Calvin replied, "Erm, erm, I must have fallen asleep. Essence, can you come and see me some time in the next few hours?"

"Why do you sound so nervous? Why are you eerming me? What's up?"

"Nothing!" he replied. "Can you come this afternoon as I need to tidy up and do a bit of work?" he asked.

"Okay, what time?"

"About three-thirty?"

"Okay, see you then," I said and the line went dead, no bye, kiss my arse, nothing!

I fumbled around the house trying to clear away from last night, my headache was horrendous, I took a few pain killers with a cuppa. I sat and wondered what Calvin would have to say, hoping it was just a misunderstanding. I have got a cheek really, I was going to dump him anyway, and I am going through with it! Or am I just saying that because I am annoyed? Of course I bloody am!

Well the time has come for me to go around to his house. I am really not looking forward to this. The drive there was long, but that's always the case when you want to find out something or want to be somewhere. I let myself in; yes, I have a key but I very rarely use it.

"Hi, Calvin, how are you?" I said through gritted teeth. "Who was that woman you were with last night?" I blurted out.

"Erm, erm, erm, just a friend," he stuttered.

"Do you hold hands and kiss all your friends like that?" I said, feeling myself getting mad.

"What? How? What do you mean?" The shock is apparent on his face.

"I saw you, Calvin! Who is she? You were both at the bus stop!"

"Where were you then? I thought that you were suffering with a really bad headache?"

"I lied! I just didn't want to see you!"

"So you lied to me. Essence, I am so sorry for what I am going to tell you."

"Well, what have you got to tell me, Calvin? I am waiting!" foot tapping away.

"Erm, never mind! Erm! No!" he stuttered.

"Calvin, grow some fucking balls and tell me!"

"Okay! Essence, just shut up and let me talk!"

My mouth fell open as Calvin has never spoken to me like that, not ever. I just sat down and shut up as he asked.

"Do you want a drink? There's some wines in the fridge."

I can still taste the wine in my mouth from last night, may as well wash it out with some more. "Thanks, yes, I will have a large glass of wine please, glass filled!"

Calvin has a whiskey in hand, he must be nervous.

"The thing is, Essence," with a big gulp of drink, "I have been seeing someone else for around six months and before her I cheated on you with a few others."

"What the fuck did you just say to me, Calvin?" I said, my face a mix of shock and anger.

"You heard me!" he replied upset yet an almost smug look appeared on his face.

I am completely gobsmacked, one, the way he is speaking to me and second the fact he has cheated on me.

"Why?" I asked. "What did or have I done to you?"

What came out of his mouth next floored me. "Look at you!" he said. "Just look at the state of you!" he carried on.

Anger just raised up in me. I slapped him in the face; he slapped me right back. "You fucking bastard!" I said to him. "When did you get so nasty?"

"I have never ever loved you, Essence, you were just there for my convenience, now I do not need you! Now get out of my house. I've said all I wanted to say." Turning his back on me."

Crying, I just ran out of his house. I got straight in my car and drove to my dad's house, I could hardly see through the tears streaming down my face.

"Dad! Dad!" Banging on the door, he wasn't there so I just sit on his doorstep waiting for him to come back. It felt like forever waiting for him to come home.

Every word Calvin said to me repeated in my head a million times. He made me feel worthless. He made me feel ugly. He made me feel worse than I have ever felt. Boring, old Calvin. No sense of style! Crap in bed! That man said these things to me. Everything I was meant to say to him! That's what was hurting me. I laughed out loud, I cannot believe he had the gall to say that to me. Who knew my ego, thought I was better than him and he wasn't worthy of me. Karma surely kicked me up the arse ha-ha.

Dad returned home. "Hello, sweetheart, I wasn't expecting you, why didn't you let yourself in?"

"It was the spur of the moment, Dad, I left my keys at home. Dad, you look tired are you okay?"

"I have just done a long shift, buttercup, I am bound to be tired."

As dad opened up the door to let us in my tears soon dried, just seeing him made me feel comforted, this man right here was the only man I needed, he is strong, he is my protector and my bestest friend.

"Let me make you a cuppa and some supper then, Dad, just go sit down. Will cheesy beans on toast do you?" I asked him.

"Yes, lovely!"

As I brought back his supper he was fast asleep on the sofa. I didn't wake him, he looked so pale and he said he was tired so I just covered him up, and I ate the cheesy beans on toast myself, I watched some TV with the sound down low, and watched him sleep. My dad has lost a little weight, he works so hard. He doesn't want to hear my troubles with Calvin so I won't bother telling him. Dad did like him a lot so I will leave it there, I will sort myself out and may tell Dad in conversation another time.

Dad woke around eleven. "Hello, sleepy head!"

"Sorry I fell asleep, darling, I am just so tired."

"I ate your supper, Dad, let me make you something now."

"No, I am going to bed, darling."

"Just a little soup, Dad?"

"No," he said, "just let me go to bed," so I gave him a hug and he said, "Your bedroom is already for you, lock up properly and go to bed yourself."

I just did as he said. I felt like a little girl again. This is just what I need, to be with my dad, at home. I went to bed, and I could hear my dad wincing, like he was in pain.

"Dad? Dad, are you okay?"

"Yes, sweet! Just got an upset stomach. It must have been something I ate at lunch!"

"But, Dad, you always take a pack up?"

"I didn't this morning because I would have been late. Can you get me a glass of water and some pain killers from the bathroom cabinet?"

As I opened it there was an array of tablets.

"Dad what are these all for? Why are there so many?" I shouted out to him.

"Oh I just haven't had a clear out, they're just old ones. Just bring the ones with the blue label." I took them to his room. He was doubled up in pain, "It's just cramp," he exclaimed. He took the tablets then settled after half an hour.

I went back to bed and thought nothing of it, he seemed okay now The bed was only a single and a bit lumpy.

The morning soon crept up. I haven't slept that well in a long while, it's probably because it's home. I made Dad and myself some breakfast, scrambled eggs and bacon for him and I just had some eggs, he skirted them around the plate.

"Dad, what's up? Why are you not eating? You must be hungry, you didn't have supper last night. Please eat your breakfast."

He forced it down. I could tell. I got dressed for the gym, as I always have some clothes at dad's, but my trainers were at my place. I went up to brush my teeth and as I was coming down I could hear him vomiting in the sink. "Dad, are you okay? Why are you throwing up?"

"I wasn't, darling, I just choked on a bit of bacon."

"As long as you are okay, Dad! You do look a little pale,. I will come back later okay. And we can have dinner together, I have made your pack up, it's in the fridge. Love you, Dad."

"Sounds like a plan to me, Love you too, sweetheart." He smiled and waved as went out the door.

I quickly get home and grab my trainers, hop in the car and head to gym. Calvin came to mind, his words burn in me. You're out of shape! Look at you! Look at the state of you! I got on that treadmill. I walked and ran. Look at the state of you! I will show you, you fucking bastard. I ran harder. I was on that treadmill for an hour. I was out of breath, and sweat poured down my face, my back was wet. I ran, out of anger, like my life depended on it, but soon enough I had to get off, I didn't even do the cool down, my legs were wobbly. I bent forward, my hands on knees, then I heard a deep voice.

"Are you all right?"

I straighten myself up and said, "Yes, thank you!" thinking it was one of the trainers. It wasn't it was the man with no name. I felt my eyes roll back, legs went to jelly and I literally fainted in his arms. Moments later I came round while still in his arms but now on the floor.

"Hello," he said. "Welcome back!"

"Hi. Sorry!" I replied, realising I'm still in his arms.

"No problem, glad that you're okay!"

"Yeah I'm fine, thank you for catching me." The nervousness in my voice so loud, I clear my throat and hurriedly get to my feet.

"Anytime, go easy." He replied with the cutest smile and off he went. I still didn't get his name. I watched him walk away, those thighs, those beautiful thighs.

"Essence, how are you feeling? Here is a glass of water." My thoughts rudely interrupted by one of the trainers.

"How do you know my name?"

"We had a look at your membership card that you dropped when you passed out and—"

"What's the guy's name that I was just with?" I interrupt. "The one that caught me?"

"I'm not too sure, when he's next in I can pass on a message for you?"

"Does he know my name?" my mind clouded with thoughts of him.

"Yes, I think he heard us call out your name, Essence I need you to sit down for a moment and have some water." The trainer replied.

"No, I'm fine, thank you. Can I get on with my workout now?"

"No, it's best you just sit for a while, then maybe go home. You've over-exerted yourself. Next time you come I will appoint a personal trainer who will help you safely achieve your body goals without you harming yourself. Give it couple of days and rest up." The trainer was right, I had over done it, my legs were still shaking and I had only just got my breath back.

I sat dazed for a moment, not quite sure what was going on, not quite sure what the hell has just happened.

"Essence, are you okay? Did you hear what he said?" another member of staff asked me.

"Erm… Yes, I am, erm, fine just a bit dazed I think."

"Okay, just take your time," she replied.

I got to my feet. "I think I'll head off now, thanks for the help."

"Do you need someone to help you out?"

"No, I'll be fine, thanks again," I replied, wanting nothing more than to leave. How embarrassing, I thought. I got to the car park and the fresh air hit me, I got into my car and just sat there gathering myself.

I decided some retail therapy is needed.

I check the time: eight-forty-five, perfect timing the shops open in fifteen minutes. I get in my car and head in the direction of the shopping centre.

I go into every shop. Every dress and skirt I try is a little tight. Who am I kidding? I couldn't get the skirts over my knees and the dresses I couldn't get over my boobs. I still brought three dresses in a size twelve, and two skirts. I will fit in them, I will. I was so determined, they will hang on the front of my wardrobe as a reminder. I went to the shoe shop next door and picked a few out. Shoes do not discriminate, they fit like a glove. Why didn't those dresses?

All this retail therapy and I still can't help but think about him, the name with no name, he held me in his arms. It may have been brief and I was out of it but yep, he held me. I was on cloud nine. I am glad I fainted today.

Chapter *Eleven*

The next day. Today is going to be a chill day. I feel like so much has happened in such a short space of time, I just need to rest and that's exactly what I'm going to do. Well, at least that's what I thought, as my phone starts ringing.

It was the hospital.

"Hello, Miss Dawson, now I don't want you to worry but your dad was admitted last night."

"What do you mean admitted and why are you only calling me only now? Two o'clock in the afternoon! What's happened? Is he okay? What's wrong with my dad?" The panic in my voice is apparent.

"As you know, your dad has been diagnosed with prostate cancer and he called last night complaining of some pain so—"

"What!" I interrupted. "No, I didn't know! Dad didn't tell me!"

"Is it possible you can come in?"

"Yes, I am on my way." I just got up off the sofa and left.

The drive to the hospital felt like a lifetime. Tears streaming down my face, I felt like I was in a daze. I finally reached the hospital. I didn't even know which ward he was on, she didn't tell me on the phone and I didn't ask. I was running around like a headless chicken panicking. A doctor saw me, "What seems to be the problem?" he asked.

"I am looking for my dad. He was admitted last night and I do not know which ward he is on, the lady on the phone didn't say!"

"Calm down, let me get you a chair," he said.

My breathing was erratic, panic stricken.

Chapter *Twelve*

I must have passed out, as I was on stretcher when I came round. "Where's my dad? I want to see my dad!"

"Miss, please calm down."

So I took a deep breath and composed myself.

The doctor asked, "What's your dad's name?"

"Claud, Claud Dawson."

"Can I ask you why he was admitted?"

"Well, the nurse said he's got prostate cancer and he had pains or something but I knew nothing about it as he never told me! How can he have cancer? Surely I would know? I see my dad every week, he didn't look ill, maybe a little tired but he looked fine!"

"In many cases people look the same as normal in the first stages. I will go find his information and get back to you," the doctor said and with a reassuring smile he was gone, and for what felt like a lifetime. I was just getting more and more frustrated and more and more upset.

The doctor finally came back. "Your dad's on the cancer ward, I will take you to him. I'm the doctor who's been monitoring him since he came in."

He helped me up off the stretcher and led me to where my dad was. "In all the upset and conversation, I never got your name," he asked obviously trying to make me feel at ease.

"Dawson, Essence Dawson," I replied.

"Nice to meet you Essence, I'm doctor Murphy.

As I neared the ward the tears were streaming down my face again. When I saw my dad he looked really poorly, laying on the bed in a foetal position, fast asleep. I just sat beside him, looking at him through my glassy eyes. I thought, not my dad, he doesn't get poorly, and he's my dad. Why did cancer choose him? He's a great dad, he hasn't been in trouble, he's never done anyone any harm. All he does is go to work, has a few drinks at home. He has never smoked.

My dad has always put me first and foremost. He is my mother and my father. My heart is absolutely breaking right now, and the ears are still streaming. I must get myself together before he wakes up. I look around for a tissue and glimpse my dad's handkerchiefs in his pocket. He was old school and always carried one, I knew he always did and I am sure he carried it for me. When I was growing up he used it for my nose, my cuts when I fell over or to wipe my mouth as I always dribbled or had food around my mouth.

He started stirring so I wiped my face and runny nose. He woke up and looked at me.

"Hello, sweetpea, who told you I was here?" He seemed shocked to see me.

"A nurse called me this afternoon, Dad."

"I told them not too."

"Why?" I asked. "Why didn't you tell me you were poorly, Daddy?"

"Essence, you haven't called me daddy for a long time, only dad."

I started to cry again. "Don't cry, Essence," he said.

"Dad, have you got cancer? They say you've got cancer! I want to hear it from you. How long have you known? Are you going to die, Daddy?" I said feeling myself becoming hysterical.

"No! Of course I'm not!" he replied with a gentle chuckle, but you could see he had fear in his eyes, and tears in front of them, of course he wouldn't let them fall.

The doctor came to his bed. Dad sat up, wincing in pain. He tried to hide it but I saw. "Mr. Dawson, can I talk to you privately?"

"No, it's fine my daughter knows now and I don't want to keep anything else from her, you can talk openly in front of her." Dad replied.

"Okay, well Mr. Dawson as you know we ran some tests when you came in last night, and the results aren't what we had hoped, I'm afraid the chemo and radiotherapy haven't worked as well as we hoped, the cancer has spread to your bones, lungs and liver, I'm sorry but there is nothing more we can do, we will carry on with pain relief to make you more comfortable"

My dad looked at me and he didn't say a word for a few minutes. The doctor was still talking but we didn't hear a thing.

"How, how long has my dad got to live?" I whispered, not actually wanting to hear.

"Your dad has two weeks, maybe three."

"What?" I said.

"Your dad has been diagnosed with cancer for over a year, and when he first came in it was already at stage four. He has done really well and listened to all our advice, taken all his meds and taken part in all the necessary treatment."

"What? No! I must not be hearing right! I would have known! I have seen my dad every week, how could you? Why would you hide it from me?"

"I am your dad, I am supposed to protect you."

"Dad, we could have done so much in that time!"

"Essence, I didn't think I was going to die. I am your protector, your dad, it wasn't supposed to be like this!" he replied, upset, the tears no longer staying his eyes.

I got up and fell to my knees. I bawled, hard. Not my dad. No, my dad can't die and leave me! "Nooo!" I cried at the top of my lungs. I stayed on that floor and I cried like a baby.

"Essence, baby please get up," my dad said so softly.

Rocking back and forth, I just couldn't control my emotions. With every strength my dad could muster he got off his bed, pain whooshing through his frail body, he let out a gasp, he looked at me and asked again, with his hand outstretched, "Please get up, darling. Please, I cannot sit on the floor beside you."

I lift my head, take his hand and get up. "Daddy, what am I to do without you?"

I gave him a cuddle, all I could feel was his bones, he had lost so much weight. How did I not see? Now I know why he wore thick overalls and big jumpers in the heat that we have been having, he was probably cold with all the weight he had lost. I kept asking, "Dad why didn't you tell me?"

"Essence, you're my little girl, why would I put this on you?"

"I am not a little girl, Dad."

"Well, you're my little girl," he said with a smile. "Darling, I am so sorry, yes I am going to leave you. I tried to do all I could to stay, that's why I didn't tell you. You're my sunshine and I didn't want to put that out."

I had no words, just tears. I looked at my dad and he looked back at me and I knew in the moment that this was real, this was really happening. My beautiful dad. My dad was dying and there is nothing I can do. I place a gentle kiss on his forehead and we hold each other.

Visiting time was nearly up. I had to leave my dad in hospital. I gave him another cuddle and he winced in pain.

"Sorry, Dad."

"I will be all right, Essence, I just need some morphine."

"I'll come back in the morning, Dad."

"What about work, you can't take time off?"

"Yes, I can and I am off for the next four days. After that I am going to take a sabbatical, I need to spend each and every last day you have left with you." He knew I had made up my mind and we left it at that.

I left and got into my car. I had forgotten to pay for parking, so I got a ticket, but just as I was tearing it off the window screen, the doctor from my dad's ward walked up to me.

"Don't worry, I will take care of that for you."

"Thank you," I said.

"I will also take care of your dad to the very end."

I just fell into his arms and started to cry. "I cannot believe my dad's going to die, I can't believe it." He just stood there holding and comforting me in the car park, I composed myself and got into my car. "Thank you again, Doctor Murphy"

"Call me Patrick." He replied

I wind my window back up and set off, driving home. On the way back I was going through all the emotions. I screamed, "Why my dad?" I held onto the steering wheel so tight that my knuckles were white, and my nails dug into the bottom of my palms. I was squeezing so hard and screaming the same, I need to get home. I soften my grip of the steering wheel, wiped my face and continued to drive.

Chapter *Thirteen*

I could barely see where I was going. Somehow I managed to get home. Opened my front door, as I closed it behind me, I locked and chained up. I headed to the drinks cabinet, vodka was staring at me. I didn't even get a glass, I just drank it from the bottle. It hit the back of my throat, a sharp burning sensation in my chest as it makes its way to my stomach Coughing and spluttering, I get a glass and some tonic. My dad would not be happy me drinking from a bottle, he brought me up better and as for drinking vodka, I never drank anything that strong in front of him. I sat on the bean bag, vodka and tonic in front of me, music playing. I drank every drop of that vodka. I went onto the whiskey after. At that moment in time I didn't care if I lived or died, my heart was broken. My dad is dying.

The realisation was wrapping me up. I started singing, at the top of my lungs, music turned right up. I tried to get up to dance but the drink made it so my wobbly legs wouldn't let me. Bang! on the walls from the neighbours so I turned down the music, good job I had a remote for the speakers, as I couldn't move.

I fell into alcohol fuelled sleep, let's face it, that was the only way I was going to sleep tonight.

After a few hours I woke. I got myself to the bathroom, just in time, but I missed the toilet completely; I threw my guts up and projectile vomited up the shower wall. I could taste every mouthful of that vodka and the whiskey. "Never again," I said to myself. I walked out of the bathroom and crawled to bed. I fell straight asleep still drunk, and I slept for another four hours.

It was seven o'clock when I awoke. My head thought it was going to explode, the pain was horrendous. Last night I needed that escape from reality but it soon hits me again as my eyes open. I will no longer have my dad in a few weeks.

I tried to eat a piece of toast, my throat would not allow it. I am going to have a shower and get dressed. In the shower I cried so much, I didn't know if it showered or my tears flowed more, my head was spinning. Surely, I am in a nightmare, my dad? No, he isn't dying.

As I was getting dressed, that's all that ran through my head. I scraped my wet hair back and got in my car, should I even be driving, my alcohol level was surely over the limit, but nothing could have stopped me from driving my car. I wind the window down, take a deep breath and start making my way to the hospital. I pulled into the car park and found a space close to the entrance and I remembered to pay my parking ticket this time. I make my way up to the ward. Dad wasn't there. "Where's my dad?" I screeched.

"He's just gone to take bath," a soft voice said to me, one that I recognised, it was Doctor Patrick.

"I will just sit and wait here then. How was he last night?" I asked,

"We had to give him extra morphine as he was in a lot of pain."

Exactly what I didn't want to hear. I'm in total shock, this still doesn't seem real. Yesterday I was told for the first time that my dad had cancer and then that the cancer has spread all over his body, and now it's just a waiting game. What the fuck!

They wheeled my dad back in a wheelchair. "Why are you not letting him walk?" I asked.

" we gave him the option and he chose the chair." The nurse pushing him answered.

Dad tried to get back into bed but nearly fell over, so the nurses helped him.

"Dad, are you all right?" I asked, feeling myself starting to well up.

"I am fine, darling," he said. I could hear the weakness in his voice.

He fell straight to sleep when he laid his head down on the pillows. I just read the paper and had a coffee. I must have read that paper front to back and back to front. Dad slept for two and a half hours. When he woke he was in pain but he couldn't have any more morphine for an hour, so he was given pain killers.

"Dad, have you eaten today?" I asked.

"No but I think I could manage a bit now."

I asked the nurse for him. She brought some soup and a few slices of bread. I helped dad sit up, still not believing he is so poorly, and so very weak. I fed him his soup. He could barely swallow, but I made sure he had half a bowl full and half a slice of bread. As he was about to lie down he threw it all up, he couldn't keep it down. I gave him a sip of water, then called the nurse.

She said, "It's his medication." I asked for the doctor. Doctor Patrick walked in and I asked if his medication is making him sick, "why does he have to have them if they're making him sick?"

What the he said next flummoxed me. "If he doesn't have those medications he will die in the next day or two." He replied.

"So what you're telling me, it's the meds that are keeping him alive?"

"Yes, Miss Dawson, basically we are giving him all kinds of pain relief, if we stop the pain relief it will make your father very uncomfortable and his body can't take much more strain, he's very weak. I'm not saying the pain will make him leave us sooner but it could be a significant contributory factor, so it's just not advisable, your dad is comfortable now and as long as we are doing that then we are doing the right thing."

I had to ring Calvin, I needed some support, I just couldn't handle all I was seeing or hearing.

Calvin's reply: "What can I do? If he is going to be here much longer? Me and you aren't together anymore Essence, I'm sorry about your dad but-?"

Anger just rose in me, so I told him, "Fuck off," and put the phone down.

I just sat and stared into space, wondering, thinking, trying to come up with some sort of plan, a miracle maybe, then I heard a whisper

"Essence, Essence." It was my dad. "When you were born everything in the sky shone like never before, the sunshine during the day, the moon and the stars during the evening. Everything was just like a whirlwind of happiness. You have brought joy to my life, Essence. Every day was so special. When I leave this life, do not cry for me, do not let sorrow drown you, live as beautiful as a butterfly. Do everything you have dreamed about, do not let anything or anyone bring you down. Darling, you are a free spirit."

Tears falling from my eyes, "I won't let you down, Daddy! I promise!" I told him.

Dad drifting back to sleep, "I love you, darling."

"I love you too, Daddy. So much." I held his hand while he fell asleep. I felt my eyes get heavy and I drifted off too, my head on the side of his arm, still holding his hand.

I slept for a couple of hours if I had known I wouldn't have closed my eyes.

Those were the last words he said to me. My Dad, my protector, my best friend was gone.

"Dad, Daddy! Wake up! They said you wouldn't leave me yet, they said we had more time!" I said repeatedly. He didn't. He couldn't. My world had just crumbled into a thousand pieces, every part of my body cried, every part of me wanted to die with him, a thousand questions I needed to ask him but now I couldn't, who do I turn to?

Chapter *Fourteen*

I left the hospital, I didn't want to leave my dad but I knew deep down that he was no longer there, he had been called home.

I needed to talk to someone, I called Aurora, we still hadn't spoken since that night, I had a go at her, but I knew she would be there for me and she didn't let me down, she came round straight away.

"Ess, I'm so sorry. I am always here for you, I always will be regardless of anything we go through, I'll always be right by your side." She said as she hugged me, tears rolling down her cheeks.

"I can't believe my dad has gone! I didn't even know he was suffering, he was my whole world."

I was saying so much to her. I could feel my mouth moving and I could see Aurora's moving but I didn't hear anything. My head was mush. My heart at the bottom of my stomach. Erratic was probably the best way to describe me. I was inconsolable.

Aurora must have been concerned as she rang my family doctors and explained what had happened and how I was. A lovely doctor soon came round, I hadn't seen her before, she spoke to me but again I didn't hear words, I just watched her mouth move. I felt myself rambling, getting louder and louder. She gave me something to calm me down, and I had to take it while she was there.

"This will help you calm down. Look after yourself, and don't hesitate to call the surgery if you need us, we have some really great support groups." The doctor said. "Stay with her for a while," she said to Aurora.

Chapter *Fifteen*

The morning arrived; in a blur I got dressed.

"Morning Es, how are you feeling?" Aurora asked in a gentle voice.//
"Like shit! I just don't know how I'm going to cope."//
"I'm always here for you, and I promise you I'm not going anywhere!"//
"Dad told me he wasn't going anywhere and he's left me." I snapped.//
"Essence I'm sorry, I- erm I've made some breakfast, you need to eat."//
"No Aurora, I'm sorry, I shouldn't snap at you like that you've been amazing. Thank you"

I sipped on a cup of coffee but to eat was the last thing on my mind, I wouldn't be able to swallow it any way. "I need to go round to Dad's house to sort through some things and make sure it's

secure," I told her.

I left Aurora at my place and made my way to Dads, I felt bad for talking to her how I did, she's just trying to help and be there for me. She's a true best friend.

As I pulled up to the house tears filled my eyes, to think I will never see my Dads face again. I walk up to the door, It was secure. Of course it was, Dad was like that. I opened it and straight away I saw a letter addressed to me; the handwriting familiar, it was Dad's. I didn't know what to expect, I stood, opened it and read it.

Dear Essence,

I am sorry I had to leave you, darling, but it was my time to go. You have made my life truly exceptional. I know you will continue to bring joy to me even in my death. I will never leave you, Essy. If you should feel a hand on your shoulder it will be me telling you that I am there and when you're in the garden planting tomatoes, I will still guide you.

Thank you, my beautiful child, you will always be my butterfly and everything that was beautiful in the world. Make me proud and achieve everything you said you were going to do.

I love you from then and still now until eternity. Do not rush to come see me, I will always be here to receive you.

Bye for now, my angel.
Love Daddy. X

All I could do was smile through my tears. My mind flicked through memories of me and him from my childhood to now, My Dad loved me just as much as I loved him.

Dad knew he wasn't going to be here for long. He had already arranged his funeral. The church. The wake. He even let my mother know to look out for me. I didn't know that he still kept in touch with her from time to time. As I walked into each room he had left an items from each year since I have been born; it was so beautiful. The house was immaculate. Another letter, left on the side table next to his chair, it was his will. He has left me everything, his house, his car and a lot of money. I sank into the, his favourite chair and I cried my eyes out. I decided right there and then I would move out of my rented apartment and move into my home, the only home I have ever known; it would let me feel Dad around me.

Chapter *Sixteen*

$\mathcal{T}$he week dragged till the day of his funeral. I wanted to but couldn't go to the chapel of rest; he wouldn't have looked the same.

I put my black dress on, and made myself look elegant, just like my Dad would want, I was ready to do this, Aurora right by side. I wasn't expecting many people to be there, my dad didn't really go out much and he never had any friends back to the house. Following the coffin, we entered the church and there must have been more than a hundred people sat watching my Dad come in. I knew none of them apart from his best friend and my dreaded mother. I looked at her. She gave me a sly smile; I just looked away, I simply hate her. I don't know her, why was she even here? Dad had even designed the order of service book for everyone. It is full of pictures of me and him, from when he was pushing me on the swing, to me playing on the beach, us fishing, us just having a good time together, always laughing, me and my hero, my Dad.

I said a few words about how much I loved him and how he was the best mum and dad I would ever have. I glanced into the pew where my so called mother was, she bowed her head when I said that, she knew that it was directed to her. Dad chose the hymn *Amazing Grace* as that was my favourite and for himself, the hymn *Morning Has Broken*, and a few prayers. It seemed to go on forever but it was only an hour. He decided to get cremated, which was a shock to me as he always wanted to be buried. I went there by myself as that's what Dad wanted. I will receive his ashes within a week.

At the wake Dad had organised to put on a magnificent buffet with a beautiful cake, he didn't want sadness. He even provided a disco, playing his favourite music and the place was decorated. He has thought of it all, he really didn't want to put anything on me, he was just perfect. All through the afternoon to the evening, everyone that was there shared their memories of Dad. Not one bad word was said, everyone loved him.

Out the corner of my eye I could see her, my mother, walking towards me. I looked straight at her, then walked away, she can fuck off, I have nothing to say to her and especially not today.

The rest of the night was a blur, everyone coming over to me giving their condolences, telling me how great he was and how much he loved me, all their faces blended together, I was answering all of them on auto pilot, I had had enough, I was ready to go home.

I decided to stay at my place tonight as it was too sombre at Dad's he wasn't there and knowing he is never going to be there again. My life will never be the same again. I have lost the only man I have ever loved and who ever loved me. I am so glad I never told him I wasn't with Calvin anymore as he would have worried who was going to take care of me. You see, my Dad only worried about me, and me alone. I was his world, he protected me, wrapped me up in cotton wool. He didn't need to know that I wasn't the goody two shoes he made me out to be. I got drunk most weekends. I did sleep around for a while when I was a teenager. I even skipped school and I forged his signature to get out of school at lunch or miss a lesson. I used to smoke in the park with Aurora. I wasn't a bad child, just a little rebel at times, like we all are. I think Dad would have laughed to be honest.

And now I'm lost.

Who am I going to call when I feel down? When I feel happy? When am I going to call him? Never! That's when.

Chapter *Seventeen*

Back in my apartment, I felt so lonely. I put my onesie on. My phone went unanswered. I smoked cigarette after cigarette. I drank so much I couldn't even see. I didn't wash. I wouldn't answer the door to anyone.

I was in that state for days maybe even weeks. Who cares anymore. I haven't had a wash or brushed my teeth. I still was in shock; my life seemed like it wasn't worth living.

Sat on my sofa, looking an absolute mess, I don't plan on leaving this position any time soon, I honestly didn't care anymore.

I never knew my dad was poorly so that's a bitter pill to swallow. I could have spent so much more time with him if he had just told me. Every part of me was angry on top of the grief and the sadness. I keep going through spells of hating him for not telling me. How can he say he didn't want to upset or bother me? That he was my protection? He took away time, time that we could have spent together making memories, laughing together, just being in each other's presence and loving each other just a little bit longer. He has hurt me so much I can't even focus.

I threw a cup across the room and shouted, "I hate you, Dad! I fucking hate you!" Coffee splattered all over the wall, the cup smashed into a hundred pieces, fuck's sake! I started to pick up the broken pieces wishing I could do that with me life.

I cut myself by accident; watching the blood flow out of me, the relief and the rush that I felt was immense. So I cut myself again. It gave physicality to the pain I felt inside. I loathed myself. I looked at myself in the mirror, and I felt nothing. I got one of my lipsticks and scrawled all over it, my reflection was so disgusting, no one will ever want me. My own dad has even left me, he didn't want me in his life either. Calvin's words repeated in my head. "Look at the state of you!" Yeah! Look at the state of me! Just look! I may as well die, no one will even know I am gone.

I pick up a bottle of vodka and start drinking it. I can't face food, I haven't eaten for a few days apart from crisps or any crap I could find, that I didn't have to cook. Alcohol was my best friend, it made me sleep, and it made me forget for a short while; the only issue, I vomited every day, my body was in a bad state, and I knew this, I just couldn't stop doing it.

There goes the door again, I didn't answer.

"Essence? Essence! I can hear you are in. Answer the door!"

It fell on deaf ears, I just sat and watched TV, well I just stared at the TV, I wasn't watching it, it was my only company, and the only company I wanted. Tears started flowing. I just couldn't help but keep bursting into tears. Every part of me keeps hurting, I have never known anyone who has died, and no one gives you a guide of how to live after it happens to you. I felt out of my depth, I have no family, it's just me, and what the fuck do I do?

I smoke another cigarette, I drink some more, I feel like I am drowning, I eventually fall asleep. When I awake vomit lay next to me, I must have thrown up in my sleep. I was on the floor in the living room. I tried to get up several times but could not move, I must have drunk so much. I look at the vodka bottle, empty, laid on its side. Surely I didn't drink it all.

"Essence," I said to myself, "what are you doing? Why are you doing this to yourself?"

My dad would be so disappointed with me, but then I don't actually care what he would think, he didn't even tell me he was dying, he made me do this, I hate him, I fucking hate him!

Crying again at the state I am in.

I find every bit of strength I have to get up. I needed the toilet. Sat on the toilet I was sick again, shitting and throwing up at the same time, not a pretty sight. I stumbled back to the living room, broken cups, empty vodka bottles and vomit strewn across the floor. I was disgusted with myself but I didn't have the energy to clean it up. I lit a cigarette and contemplated taking my own life. I was in the depth of sadness, who would miss me anyway? I was losing weight though ha-ha not that that matters, fucking look at me! The bags under my eyes were protruding, and although I had lost weight my stomach was swollen, my eyes were red and bloodshot from all the crying. I could even smell the stench of my breath, a mixture of vodka and vomit; my whole body was so weak and at the end of its tether. My hair flat to my forehead with grease. Somehow I make it back into the bathroom, open the bathroom cabinet. I knew exactly what I was looking for, a bottle of pills were now in my hand, I walk back to the living room, I say walk, stagger is more appropriate. I go to the drinks' cabinet, grab whatever bottle there was and poured myself a drink and laid the tablets out on the coffee table.

I take a sip of my drink, then swallow a tablet. I ask myself what am I doing, but I continue, a drink, a tablet, a drink, another tablet, I must have taken half the bottle of these tablets then there was a knock at the door.

"Go away!" I shouted.

"Essence it's me, Calvin, open the door."

"Go away!" I said in a faint voice, starting to feel the effect of the tablets and alcohol. "Just leave me alone!"

"Open the door!" he shouted again.

I think I blacked out.

"Essence! Essence! What have you done?" Calvin begged, shaking me. I opened my eyes slightly; he slapped my face gently, and I was gone.

Next thing I woke to noise, I was in an ambulance on the way to the hospital. I could hear people talking around me, but I couldn't open my eyes. They gave me something to make me vomit and put me on a drip as I was severely dehydrated. I was in and out of consciousness. Darkness again.

I half opened my eyes. I was now in the hospital, gowned up and hooked to some machine. Calvin was sitting by my bedside.

"What are you doing here?" I croaked.

"Can't you remember, I got you here"

"What do you mean, you got me here?"

"I found you, Essence."

I fall back to sleep. I woke about an hour later. Feeling a little stronger. Calvin was still there.

"Calvin, just go home, I am not your girlfriend anymore, and you do not have to look after me!"

"Essence, were you trying to kill yourself?"

"No, I wasn't, I was just…"

"Just what, Essence?" he said. "What do you think your Dad would say?"

I burst out crying as I knew what he was saying was true, would I let him know he was speaking the truth, never. I suck my tears back up. He is one of the reasons I feel so low, he broke up with me, and used those nasty words to hurt me, Mr. Boring did that to me. Mr. Fucking Boring said all them things to me. That hurt me more.

"How did you get into my house?" I asked him.

"I've still got a key and I am glad I do! The door was chained, I had to smash through that but, Essence…"

"You did what?" I said, interrupting him.

"That's the only way I could get in, don't worry I will fix it for you."

"There is no need!" I said to him. "Haven't you got a girlfriend to look after, why are you even bothered about me?"

"Listen," he said, "we were together for a while, I still care about you."

"How the hell do you still care about me, Calvin? Can you remember those horrible things you said to me? Do you remember, you slapped me? In all the time we were together you never shouted at me, not once!" I could feel myself getting upset again.

"I am sorry," he said. "I didn't mean to hurt you, I really didn't, that's the last thing I ever wanted. Anyway you slapped me first." The room falls silent and we just look at each other. I saw a look in his eyes that I hadn't seen for a while.

"Essence, I have made a mistake, will you—"

The doctor arrived, so Calvin didn't get time to finish his sentence. The doctor was the same one who looked after my dad, Doctor Patrick.

"Hello again Essence!" he said. "do you mind telling me what were you thinking, doing this to yourself?"

"I wasn't thinking, I knew exactly what I wanted, I wanted to die and that feeling still hasn't left me. All I can see is darkness. I have no one. No one to love. No one to love me. No one who would miss me!" That's when I just went into a deep silence, realising I probably said too much, but feeling a release that I had spoken them into the air Doctor Patrick and Calvin were talking to me but I never said another word.

"I am going to refer you to someone who can talk to you about all you are going through, Essence but in the meantime you will be staying here for a couple days. Your body has taken a beating with all the alcohol and tablets. You don't seem to have eaten either so we will be keeping an eye on you. I will be back to see you tomorrow," Doctor Patrick said and then he left.

"Thanks, Doctor," Calvin said. "I will stay with her for a while longer."

I just wanted to scream at him "Go away, I don't need you! I don't need anyone!" but I couldn't mutter a word. I could feel myself in that dark, empty abyss of my soul and it was where I wanted to be. I couldn't see an end to how I was feeling.

Calvin eventually got up to leave.

"I will be back tomorrow, Essence, I will not go away until you can see there is life and light after your dad's death, I won't let you do this yourself," and with a rueful smile he left.

One of the nurses bought me something to eat. I just pushed it around the plate. It didn't touch my lips; I was just physically incapable of eating. I did however drink the tea and it felt nice to feel the warmth in my stomach.

I will try and eat something in the morning if my body will allow it, but right now it's too much too soon.

All through the night I was being checked on, even when I was asleep they would come to wake me to see if I was all right. Yes, I would be if you just let me sleep. As the morning arrived so did breakfast. Nope I still couldn't bring myself to eat anything. I do feel okay though with the drip and I was drinking tea and water.

I have lost a stone in weight, It's grief weight loss. but I look awful, the bags under my eyes are grey, my skin is dry and I look like I could sleep for fifty years.

Calvin polled up again, and he has brought me some tomato soup, it's my favourite when I feel poorly or had a cold, It would always make me feel better. I cannot believe he even remembered. It was in a flask so was still nice and hot. He poured some in a cup and I sat up and I sipped it. It was just what I needed.

Calvin was talking about Jane, his girlfriend. "She is the total opposite of you, Essence. She makes me do everything because she is pregnant, the only break I get is when I go to work."

I honestly couldn't care less, so I just sat and listened, it was nice to hear that he wasn't happy.

"Please, Essence, say something."

I didn't utter a word. He just kept bleating on. I thought to myself, you made your bed now lie in it.

He said she almost lost the baby and how he really wanted her to. I thought that was a cruel thing to say even for him. I don't know who he is anymore, he is not the man I once knew. He's direct disrespectful, arrogant, all the things I hate in a human being.

I work with someone like him, Troy. Arrogant cocky fucker. He's been at the firm since he left school, longer than all of us. He smokes like a chimney; always outside puffing away. He has never moved up from the position he started with. You see, the bosses know he is incapable, but he thinks he could do their jobs. He goes around giving everyone orders but no one takes a blind bit of notice apart from the newbies; he lords it up in front of them all. The posting which he should be doing, putting them in everyone's post boxes, he gets them to do. We also heard he's been stealing stationery, pens and anything that can be lifted. Stamps are his thing, and he will take one or two off different desks at different times. He is a married man. He had an affair with a woman called Lophie, she's a right jealous bitch but I am not going to bleat on, only that she's into the habit of taking other women's men. She has children, three boys, but it's not talked about, she's a story for another day. I heard that Troy is going to get sacked as he ordered double the amount of stationery but only gave half to the company so he's under fraudulent inquiries, but yeah, he is an arrogant, disrespectful prick, like the man sitting beside me right now.

Anyway, here I am lying in bed in hospital, and I have Calvin who just won't leave. I do appreciate the soup but I want him to go now. I get a bit of paper and pen. I write a little note to the nurse to get rid of him.

She seemed to take ages to get here, not like last night when they were every five minutes, or so it seemed.

When she finally arrives I put the note in her hand while she was putting the blood pressure monitor on. My pressure was fine. She walked off but came back within five minutes. She told Calvin that I need my rest now so if he could come back another time.

"Of course," he said. "See you tonight then, Essence."

Oh for crying out loud when will he get the message to leave me alone. I thanked the nurse and she said with a smile, "Oh, you can speak then!"

I smiled and said, "Yes."

I was probably alone for about an hour before Lucy came to see. Calvin must have told her I was here. I didn't mind, I guess I needed a friendly face. She sat with me for a while and listened to everything I had done and how I felt. She agreed with what the doctor had said and persuaded me that the right thing to do was to speak with a counsellor. I felt a little weight had been lifted off my shoulders. She brought me lunch as well, and I maybe ate half of it. It's crazy to think how a little conversation can make you feel, she is such an amazing friend. Eventually Luc had to go, she had to be at work.

The nurse came in to do her checks. "I've got to say I'm sweating a lot!" I said

"That will be the Delirium tremens or D.T's as you've probably heard it referred to. You're sweating out all the alcohol you have consumed over the last few weeks. It will soon pass," she replied.

"My stomach is cramping up terribly, is there anything I can have to take the edge off?" I asked.

"I will speak to the doctor and see what we can do. I'll be back soon."

"Thank you."

I was in so much pain more than I made out but I didn't say a word, I deserved it the way I was talking about my dad. I really didn't mean it. I was and I still am angry that he didn't tell me he had cancer for as long as he did but I know I must forgive him as I can't carry on like this or I will be joining him. I know deep down I don't want to die, and somehow I must muster up the courage to say thank you to Calvin as he saved my life.

I told the nurse to let Doctor Patrick know that I was ready to speak to someone about everything, and that the sooner the better.

Chapter *Eighteen*

THE NEXT DAY

So the time came for me to see the counsellor.

Doctor Patrick didn't mess around he got someone in to speak to more or less straight away, and she seemed lovely but then again in her role I guess I should expect no less.

She let me do all the talking. It was a lot easier than I thought. I blurted everything out. How I was devastated about my dad dying and that he didn't tell me he was having treatment for over a year. It wasn't fifty-fifty when you have stage four cancer, the odds are less; it was like he had died twice. I just couldn't shake the anger I felt, would I be able to forgive him for that betrayal.

The counsellor asked me, "Do you think that your Dad intentionally wanted to hurt you? Or did he protect you from the actual pain and anguish he was going through? Do you think he didn't want you to see him throwing up and doubled up from how much pain he was in? Do you really think he wanted to hurt you, Essence?"

I simply just wept like a baby at that moment; she was right, she made me question everything I thought. I realised that Dad would never want me to see him like that and he was protecting me as always. I felt so ashamed of myself, how could I have even sink so low to believe my beautiful Dad would hurt me?

"Now, Essence, I want you to take a deep breath. Do you want to carry on with this session?"

"Yes, I do."

"Okay, so, Essence, tell me, have you got any other family, any siblings?"

"Stepbrothers and sisters but I have never met them."

"Why is that, Essence?" she asked.

"Because they're my mother's children and I hate her," I seethed "Do you want to talk about it?" she asked gently.

"I will be here all day, I haven't anything good to say about her."

"I have cleared my day for you, Essence, so please go ahead."

"My dad brought me up from the age of five -"

"Essence, I want to hear about your mum?"

"She is no Mum of mine! She gave birth to me, that's about it. Dad told me she was so excited when they were pregnant with me. When I was born she wouldn't let anyone hold me, she said I was so fragile, even though I was eight pounds ten ounces. She just wanted me all to herself. Everywhere she went she took me with her. She brought me the most beautiful dresses and shoes to match; she spoilt me so much. Dad had to tell her to slow down as I was growing out of the clothes before I'd even wore them. She brought me every Disney movie on video. She never talked to me in a baby voice, she talked to me properly. She always said how clever I was and wanted to make sure I spoke properly when I got to school. She absolutely worshipped the ground I crawled and walked upon. I started nursery at three and they would have to basically tear me out of her arms----Then she started a part time job and that's when everything changed. She would go out all the time and leave me with Dad. She never took me to nursery anymore and Dad took over everything she did, and then when she could spend time with me it was never nice, it was just rushed. We never sat for a meal together and her and Dad argued constantly. Mostly her shouting at the top of her voice. I would sometimes hear Dad crying in his room when she was on one of her many nights out.

I was two weeks away from my fifth birthday and she had packed all her bags and left. I didn't understand. I was so young, each and every evening after Dad put me to bed I could hear him, he was so upset but when I would ask him he would make some excuse and say he was fine.

After she had gone my dad made sure my childhood was an adventure, he took me on holidays. Our garden was lovely, he showed me how to grow vegetables, he taught me how to fish, he taught me how to do everything. He was my mum and dad. The day she left

I never saw her again. I am in my late twenties now and that woman has never got in touch with me. The reason she left. Because she was seeing another man, for a couple of years too before dad found out. It absolutely broke his heart, it took him a very long time to get over her. But he did, he never understood why she did it, as he thought they were happy.

"At school everyone else had a Mum, and I never understood why I didn't, but to be honest, like I have stated before, I never missed out on anything. When Dad found out she had two children with that the man she left him for, he was devastated. How could she bring up two other children and not want her first born? That's when he decided to send every card or present she sent right back to her. He would buy me presents; he didn't want anything from her. That's one of the things Dad didn't shield me from; he told me everything from the age of ten and asked how I felt about it. I just didn't care by then.

"Seeing her at Dad's funeral was the first time I'd clocked eyes on her from the age of four. I knew it was her as Dad kept some pictures in a drawer. She just looked older. I was absolutely livid that she had the audacity to sit at my Dad's funeral. I can never see us ever getting on, she is a stranger and so are her children to me. I have probably walked past them a million times, it's not their fault as they don't know anything about me either. I did often think how nice it would have been to have a sister, but in hindsight I always did in Aurora, she's both my best friend and my sister. I am only just starting to talk to her again as not long before my dad died we exchanged a few words, as I was sick of her using me, but as soon as I picked up the phone about Dad she was there for me. No doubt, she is with her sugar daddy I'm not one of those girls who goes after a man for money, I will choose love every time. Aurora likes the fine things in life, and that's because she has always had it, her Dad is very rich. and that's why she goes for these type of men, but how the hell can anyone lay with a man for their money surely, your self-respect is more important. I do not care what you have as long as you care for me. Just like my dad cared for me, love will always be more important." I rambled on and on, I think I went off on a bit of a tangent, but it felt good to get all that off my chest.

"Thank you, Essence, it seems to me you had so much more on your plate than just your Dad's death. You seem to have buried a lot of anger and disappointment from quite a few of your friends and family. I am going to recommend that you are safe to go home tomorrow from a counselling perspective, obviously medically that's up to them, but we will have another session in the morning to make sure"

"Thank you so much, you don't understand how much better I feel."

"My pleasure, Essence, I will see you at some point tomorrow."

I went back to my bed. I felt a huge release and know now for sure I need to tell anyone who thinks they can treat me badly that they can't even if I lose them on the way.

My mother is a different story, it's going to take a lot longer as I can't see myself with her in a room or anywhere for that matter, never mind talking to her. How am I supposed to get past all those years? She hasn't even come to mind before now, I didn't realise that she was causing me an issue, I don't even know her. Yes, she gave birth to me; yes, she looked after me for nearly five years; but I was her child, her girl, her first born and she abandoned me and my dad. She hurt him so much. He loved her, so much so that he never had another relationship with anyone.

Oh gosh! When I think about it now, my dad dedicated his whole life to me, like his *whole* life! How selfish was I blaming him for not telling me he was poorly? I will never forgive myself for cutting and nearly killing myself, how could I have tarnished his memory like that? My Dad would have been so disappointed in me. I promise myself and my Dad that from this moment on I will do everything I have set out to do. I have taken a sabbatical from work for a while and I'm going to extend it so it's for a year. I need to focus on me and my future and the next steps I need to take. I want to be that strong, independent woman my dad brought me up to be. I have wasted the time off that

I have had already. I am ready to go home now, ready to become the new, stronger me.

"One more night, just one more, Essence" I say to myself. Just as I am putting my life in order in my head, it's visiting time. I'm not expecting any visitors though, but of course, in walks Calvin. To be fair no one knows I am here apart from him and Lucy and that's the way I want it to stay. I do not want my business to be the gossip of the town.

"Calvin, haven't you got anything better to do?"

He leans in for a kiss on the cheek. I move my face back. "What are you doing? You don't get to kiss me in any way."

"Sorry, Essence, I thought—"

"You thought what?" I exclaimed. "Calvin, we are not together anymore and that was your choice. You have got another woman now, and with a baby on the way."

"Things are not working out between me and her."

"And what's that got to do with me? As I said, you made your choice and it was behind my back. What about the other women you slept with? I was really taken aback by that. That you could do that to me, Calvin!" The upset in my voice takes me by surprise.

"They were one night stand.! I was getting all this attention from these women and I couldn't believe it so I took the leap and I regretted it straight away."

"Is that why you did it again? What made you stay with that bitch you're with now Calvin?"

"Well…" he said, "I think she trapped me by getting pregnant. She knew I was with you and she thought if she got pregnant I would stay and I felt obliged to do so. It's been a living hell, living with her."

"But you still have your place?" I asked, a little perplexed as to why he is telling me all this.

"Yes I have, I am not that stupid to give it up as I have always known she is not you, Ess."

"Calvin, you may as well stop there as I am not taking you back. You think that you can just swan in, with your soup and apologies and think I will just take you back? All because your life is fucked and you've realised the grass isn't greener? Not a chance! You can go now!"

"Ess! Please just listen–"

"No! Please just leave me alone. I have just lost my Dad, Calvin, you are the last thing on my mind right now. I never did tell him about how you dumped me or how you slapped me. He liked you!"

"Essence, you slapped me first. It was just a reaction."

"Listen, I forgive you, please just leave me be, I really don't have anything else to say you."

"Okay, I will go now then. Essence, can I come and see you tomorrow?"

"You can come here, Calvin, but I won't be here. I am hoping to get out of here tomorrow and I won't be at home either."

"Please, Essence, can I call you then?" he begged.

"For god's sake! Why? I have seen you so much more in the last few days than I ever did when we were together. Leave it for a while then call me. But as I have said, I am grieving for my Dad, so any problems you have I cannot help you with. If you do or don't want to be with that woman then you need to work it out but it's not my issue. But there is one thing I want to know, you said she knew you were with me? Does she know me?"

"No, she has seen us together though in our local."

"What did you say? She has seen us together in our local?"

He repeated it again.

"What? So she planned on taking you away from me? Did you know that's what she was doing? As you work with her as well, don't you?" The plot seems to be thickening, "Well? did you?"

He went silent.

"Answer the bloody question!" I shouted.

"Okay! Okay! Yes, I suppose I did. She was always around me at work, bringing me coffee and cakes, and after a while I was flattered, as she chose me and not any of the other guys, as a few of them did fancy her. But I swear to you, Essence, I never even gave her a glimpse before that. She came onto me and—"

"And you fell for it, hook, line and sinker."

"I cannot say sorry enough, Ess, if I could take—"

"Calvin, like I said, it's too late. That woman is the kind of woman I despise, the kind of woman who will see another couple happy and want to have a piece of it, well in her case all of it, she more than likely targeted other couples as well and now she's pregnant! Or was that planned? She took you from me Calvin and she made sure she would keep you. And you are the fool that fell for it and now you're telling me you don't want her? Well there's a thing! I don't know what to say to you, Calvin."

Quiet falls over the room. I think he got the message; he just sat looking at me, his eyes filled with sorrow. I couldn't feel sorry him, I was so upset with him and I couldn't take him back, I couldn't let him take me back to that place of darkness. Right now I really could do without him being here but I must thank him before he goes, although he did play a part in my demise.

"Calvin, thank you for saving my life," I said once I calmed down, breaking the tension that had descended.

"You're welcome! I hated seeing you like that and I am glad you've found your voice. and I've cleaned up your place, it was in a right state. I found so many vodka bottles, coffee up the walls and broken cups, you vomited pretty much everywhere in that house and I've fixed the door. Ess, I am so sorry I didn't support you when your Dad passed. I didn't realise how bad it had affected you I was an arsehole, I knew you two were close I was a selfish prick." You could hear the sadness in voice.

I started to feel something, I don't know if it was guilt for shouting at him, but in this moment a twinge of something was there for him, but I wouldn't let it show.

"Why would you? We weren't together, you hadn't seen me. You had moved on, and you didn't care."

"Please, Ess! I am truly sorry, I should have been there for you, and I did care. I do care! We were together for so long and I let you down." He pleaded.

"That should have stood for something but it didn't. You hurt me, Calvin, you were so mean to me. I would never have thought you of all people would have spoken to me that way or did the things you have done."

"I cannot apologise any more, Essence, we need to put it all that behind us, we need to get past all of this, you need to move on."

"Calvin, my Dad has died, how do I get past that? He was the only person that loved me."

"I love you too, Essence!"

"You know what I mean, my Dad has been in my life, all my life. I turned to him about everything and anything, his love was unconditional."

"Have you seen any of your friends through all this, Essence?"

"Nope, I tried to cope on my own and as you can see I didn't... Calvin, please go home now, I will call you tomorrow. I need to rest. I am seeing the counsellor again tomorrow, I will let you know how it goes." I'd had enough of the toing and froing of this conversation.

"Okay. Night, Ess, talk tomorrow," he said as he got to feet.

Calvin finally left.

Chapter *Nineteen*

I gazed out of the window, the afternoon slowly turning into night. The man with no name came into my thoughts and I swear he said, "I am glad you are all right." It can't be him but I didn't care whether it was or not. He made me want to get well.

Just as that thought came to me the nurse walked in. Perfect timing, because my gosh I was hungry, my stomach was gurgling, so I ask her if I could have something to eat. She brought me a sandwich.

"I can't eat this," I said to her. "The bread is stale, only a duck could eat that! Can I have something hot, please?"

She was very abrupt with me. "I have given you something to eat, and if you can't eat that then you will have to wait like everyone else. Dinner will be served in an hour."

"I'm starving. Please can I have something to eat now? Some soup so I dip the sandwich in?

"Miss Dawson, like I said dinner will be here in an hour and you must wait like everybody else." She turned on her heel and left.

"Wow!" I thought, I wasn't rude to her, impatient maybe, but not rude.

Dr Patrick was with another patient adjacent to me. He must have heard what was said, and had a word with the nurse, because within thirty minutes there was a plate of hot food on the table in front of me. Shepherd's pie and loads of vegetables, plus a pudding. I ate every single bit of it. I just needed a drink but didn't dare ask that nurse, so I went to the bathroom and got some water. As I came back Doctor Patrick was at my bed looking at my chart.

"Hello, Doctor Patrick," I said to him, feeling myself blushing. Why was I blushing? I must have looked a mess.

"Hello, Miss Dawson, and how are you feeling?"

"Please call me Essence. I am feeling so much better, thank you. I never got to say, or at least I don't think I said, thank you so much for looking after my dad."

"You're welcome," he said. "That's what I am here for."

"Yes, I know but you went above and beyond. So thank you," I reiterated.

He smiled. "Essence, I've heard you're hoping to go home tomorrow? You have been through a great ordeal. From a medical perspective I see no reason why you can't go home, and as you know the counsellor is also happy for you to go, but I need to know if we let you go tomorrow there won't be a repeat and you will continue with the counselling?"

"I promise you, Doctor Patrick, I will be fine. I have already turned over a new leaf in my book of life," I said, the tone in my voice optimistic and determined. I honestly meant it too.

His facial expressions softened at that moment. He was looking at me not like a doctor anymore. "Miss. Dawson?"

"Essence, I said,

"I would like to ask you out for dinner. I know I am not supposed to, being your doctor and all, but there is something about you. I was drawn to you from the very first time I saw you, and there was never an appropriate time to ask you. The time is probably not right still but if you don't ask you will never know."

I was taken aback as every time I saw him I looked like trash, but yet here he is asking me out. "Yes! I, I mean I would like that. But can I get out of here first?" I replied, blushing again.

He gave me his card and said, "Call me when you're ready, there really is no rush, as you still need to rest."

I lay back on to the bed and thought, things are really looking up. I was alive. I was full. I got asked out. I'm going to the counsellor, and she has made me see there is life after my Dads death. I've told Calvin about himself and I stood my ground. I'm a little bit proud of myself in this moment. I will always miss my Dad, and I will love him unconditionally for the rest of my life, but no more drowning my sorrows, I need to live my life as he would want me to.

I closed my eyes and drifted to sleep. In comes the man with no name. He picked me up and sat me down in a field full of flowers. I felt like a princess. Looking up to the sky, it was as blue as far as the eyes could see. It was so romantic. He kissed me so gently like he knew I was fragile. I didn't want to wake up from this dream.

Chapter *Twenty*

Waking up I feel so ready to face the world. My dad told me to do everything I set out to do and I will, not just for him but for me too.

I got up, got washed and dressed, starting the day right. My breakfast came, scrambled eggs, sausages and toast, followed up with some fruit.

"Right, Essence, let's do this" I said to myself.

Time to go to counselling.

"How are you feeling today, Essence?"

"I am feeling good, thank you. I can see a better outlook in my life. I am going to take everything step by step. I can't believe I tried to do that to myself, I just didn't see another way but I do now and I have so much to live for. I will not let anyone make me feel that low ever again or allow myself to get so deep without speaking to someone."

"You will get my full support that you are ready to go home but be sure to know that you will need to keep up with these meetings. Right now you are strong and feeling positive and I don't want that to slip and we end up with you back in here again, so once you get home and settled call me to arrange another appointment. Here's my card. Take care of you, Essence."

"Thank you again, for just listening to me and allowing to just rant and cry, and well you know, I honestly can't put into words how I feel already. I know it's your job but yeah, I'm rambling aren't I? I said laughing.

The counsellor chuckled. "It's okay Essence and you're welcome. I'll be expecting your call."

Chapter *Twenty-one*

I decided to walk home. The fresh air welcomed me. I took a deep breath and said a grateful. "Thank you, thank, you, for welcoming me back." I took everything in. I appreciated the trees, touched every flower I walked past. I could actually hear every bird singing, the bees buzzing, butterflies fluttering. I just saw a bright and beautiful beginning.

I got home and Calvin was there. "Give me my keys, thank you. I told you I would call you. Just leave, Calvin, this is far too soon." I had to tell him. The audacity.

He gave me back my keys without a word and he left. There and then I packed up my clothes and personal things. I would need to get boxes for everything else but that can wait for a moment I got in my little car and drove to my Dad's, my old, new home, and dropped the clothes off. I managed to get hold off some boxes, Dad had some in the loft, my perfect Dad, always prepared for everything and anything, there was 30 in total. I went back to my place and I rang around for a removal van, and for the first time not for prices but for availability, I wanted to be out of here, I was ready for a fresh start.

Van sorted, it would be here in the morning, and with that I was on a mission packing, and I didn't stop until I was finished.

Looking around my apartment I reflected on the memories made here, there weren't that many in all fairness or none important enough to talk about, I would miss it here though, simply because this was where I moved to when I left home, my first place, and I never thought I would be leaving it to go back.

I sat and had a cup of tea and said goodbye to the old me. One last sleep here then I was going home to the family home.

It was getting late so I got into bed. I didn't sleep very well, maybe a few hour. I woke at half four so I packed the very last bits, my kettle, my cup and spoon. One last shower, and I was ready for the move. I had to wait for four hours for the removal men to get here but that soon came around, as they loaded up the van I drove to my family home., It's crazy when you sit back and think about it, your life packed into cardboard boxes and chucked in a van. I smile. I'm happy and I feel free.

I got home, I opened the door and I could smell my dad. Tears trickled down my face; a calm hit me. It was like Dad was saying, "You're home now, darling, you're home."

Another letter from him on the table in the kitchen, I felt his kiss on my forehead.

Do all you have dreamt of, never let anything in life drag you to the earth. Grow like the beautiful flower you are, the most beautiful flower in any field, wild but yet so devastatingly beautiful, you could never grow in a garden. You are in every field and land, all over. I will love you my child, for always. All My Love Dad xx

I just dropped to my knees and prayed to God, to please look after my Dad, I already knew he was at peace. He just came to me to make sure I would be too.

As my things started to arrive I asked them to put everything in each room. Everything was labelled for bathroom etcetera. Dad only had essentials, so everything fit into place; just his bed to be removed and mine to be put in its space. I did one room at a time, and never stopped until it was done. It took me about six hours. I will paint and change the colour scheme at some point but there is no rush. It's only five so I think I will go to the gym in a shorty, but first a little to eat

Chapter *Twenty-two*

I must have done too much. I opened my eyes and it was bright out. Did I sleep all the way through? To be honest I'm not surprised, the last however many nights' sleeps have either been alcohol induced or disturbed. It was nice to fall asleep naturally, and to feel so close to my dad. I'm in a good mood again today, ready to face whatever I may encounter. Quick shower, coffee and then to the gym.

Looking through my handbag to find my gym membership I found the card Doctor Patrick had given me. I pondered whether to call him. Is it too soon after dad's death? Too soon since leaving the hospital? I knew my dad would tell me to go for it, especially if he would have known about everything that happened with Calvin. I deserved some fun, surely?

I plucked up the courage to call him. As soon as he answered I put the phone down, I was so nervous. I gave myself five minutes, took a deep breath and rang again, and this time I spoke, well I say spoke, I stuttered,

"Hi, it's Essence."

"Hello!" he said. "I was hoping you would call, how are you?"

"I am fine, Doctor"

"Please, call me Patrick."

"Ha, sorry. So, Patrick, do you still want to go on that date?" I can't believe I just blurted that out. I was changing.

"Yes, of course," he replied. "Are you free tonight?"

"Erm, erm yes I am free," I said, shocked and excited. I wasn't expecting it to be so soon.

"I will pick you up at eight?"

"Can I ask where we are going, Patrick? So I can dress accordingly."

"I will send you the details, Essence. Just text me your address and I will see you later."

"Okay, see you later."

"Bye." Then the line went dead.

Six o'clock, time to get ready.

I was beside myself with excitement, he sent me the details. We are going for a meal at a French restaurant up town. I fetch out a few dresses from the closet, but I didn't want to overdo it, so classy it is. The green, one shoulder dress didn't fit, still a little bit too snug, but I had another classy number. I had forgot I'd lost over a stone in weight due to all the stress I had been under, and the lack of food, not that I am happy I had to go through what I did, but I am buzzing I am a stone lighter.

Strapless black number with a small frill around the hem, garden green shoes and bag, it was one of the smaller sizes in my collection. I shower and scrunch my curls. I take my time to apply my makeup. I slip into my dress, which fits perfectly, shoes on and a simple chain, I was ready half an hour before he got there.

I am so nervous. I pace the floor and look into the mirror for the tenth time, check my breath, extra mouth wash I think, just to be sure and I apply more lip gloss. A knock on the door jolted me. I straighten myself up, one last look in the mirror.

I answer the door.

"*Wow*!" was the first word he said. "You look beautiful!" His eyes lit up.

He looked dashingly handsome, dressed to perfection. His dark blue eyes, almost black, blue, looked at me from my feet all the way up until our eyes locked. I really wanted to kiss him. "Essence!" I said in my head. "Get a grip you've only just met this man."

He opened the car door for me; no one has ever done that. As his driver – yes, he had a driver – took us to the restaurant he spoke to me about himself, his voice as calm as the ocean on a summer's day. I felt at ease with him. I just listened with the occasional yes. I probably spoke more but I was drowning in his voice.

At the restaurant he asked me what I would like. I just said, "Surprise me!" and that's just what he did. I like foreign food but I had never tried French. It was delicious; we even had champagne. I was careful not to consume too much though.

We never stopped talking, he told me of his travels abroad about how Jamaica was so relaxed that he never wanted to come home, and how much he loved India for all the exotic foods, the wildlife safari in Africa seeing all the big, beautiful animals roaming free, walking right up to them in the jeep, and how he instantly fell in love with Hawaii so much so that he brought his own place out there, the beauty of the people and the scenery captured him, "Maybe one day we can go together Essence." A bit soon I thought to myself, I've only just met you, but I smiled and nodded. There was no awkward moments, it was like it was meant to be. The evening soon came to an end. He insisted on taking me home. He walked me to the front door, and that kiss I was longing for at the beginning of the date, he gave to me. It was so tender, and only lasted a few seconds. The night couldn't have ended any better.

"I will call you," he said as he was leaving.

All I could say was, "Okay." I still felt his lips on mine.

I went straight to bed. I slept like a baby, I was on cloud nine.

I woke to a message on my phone. '*Thank you for last night, it was amazing, can I see you again tonight? Patrick x.*'

I thought that was a bit quick. I sat on that text for a while as I didn't want to seem too eager. I gave it half an hour, then texted back, ha-ha I was eager. 'Yes, I would love too, where are you thinking?'

"I got hold of a pair of tickets to watch the ballet, Swan Lake?"

I have never been, so I was excited to try new things. The day seemed to drag. Aurora called, we had a brief chat but I wasn't really wanting to converse with her as I was still a bit upset about how she has treated me but I know she was there for me when I needed her so I did arrange to meet her later in the week and I told her about Patrick.

The nerve of her, she said, "I must meet him, he sounds like a catch." Just because he is a doctor she saw pound signs.

I just said, "I will see you at some point in the week," I made my excuses and put the phone down.

To make the day go faster I went to the gym. I did a great work out and then went for a swim. The man with no name entered as I was leaving. He said, "Hello, how are you feeling after your fainting episode a while back?"

"I'm fine now thank you," I said hurriedly and left him standing there, I hope I didn't come across rude though but to be honest with seeing Patrick I haven't really thought about him, but it was really nice of him to ask. On my way home I went to Choc Chip and had a bite to eat, with my favourite hot chocolate of course.

I look out the window and saw that bus stop where I saw Calvin and that conniving bitch Jane sitting. I hated him all over again, then a smile came over my face. "Just get over it, Essence, you're going out with the doctor in a few hours." As I got home I thought about what I should wear tonight, it's not like *Pretty Woman* when she went to the theatre so I looked it up on Google; smart casual it is then.

He picked me up as he did yesterday only this time we had champagne on the way. The way he looked at me at first was flattering but it was starting to become off putting, but I just brushed it off, it was probably just me overreacting, I haven't done the whole "date" thing in a while. As we were walking towards the theatre doors he held my hand. I quickly let go as it was only our second date; just because I let him kiss me, we were hardly an item.

I really enjoyed the ballet, it was so moving and told a story with every pirouette.

As the evening was drawing to an end Patrick asked me, "Can I see you again tomorrow?"

I said, "No," as I already had plans.

"That's fine," he replied, but his face told a different story.

Again I thought, it's just me looking too much into things. As I arrived home, he went in for a kiss and I gave him my cheek.

"Night, Patrick. Thank you for tonight."

"Night Essence."

I turned and went inside, locked my door and chained it behind me. I did feel a bit uneasy but also thought, as I said before I haven't dated for a while, almost three years, I wasn't even doing the whole dating thing before I met Calvin. I was just happy being single and me and him just happened, so this is how it must be.

The next day I received the biggest bouquet of flowers and an invitation out although I'd already said no. I gave him a text and said, 'Thank you for the flowers but I cannot go out tonight as I told you last night.' I didn't get a text back for quite a few hours, he must be back at work today.

I decide to pop into work to see everyone, not like I've got anything else to do. As soon as I got there everyone pounced on me to see how I was and to tell me the gossip, but first I wanted to speak to my boss, Michael. He was looking a bit drawn but was more concerned about me. I was sick of talking about me so I turned the tables. "Are you okay?" I asked.

"Well, with my wife wanting to leave me, I am on top of the world!" I knew he was being sarcastic. "I did her wrong, Essence, she found out Amanda was having my child."

"What, you and Amanda? As in your PA Amanda?"

"Don't play me for a fool, Essence, I know you knew about me and her, everybody in this place does. I can't just sack her either, on what grounds can I do that? My wife thinks I should and that she will not even consider continuing in a marriage until she has gone. Even if I could, Amanda is carrying my child, she will be permanent person in my life. So it's a no win for me no matter what I do."

"I'm sure you will sort it, Michael, if you really want to. Anyway, I came in to see if I could come back to work, just take six months rather than a year. I need something to focus on, something that I really enjoy and most of my friends are here."

"Essence, you would be doing not only yourself a great help but you would be doing me a big favour."

"I still have two months to go then I will be back, thank you. Do not forget, Michael, I am only a phone call away if you need me."

"That's fine," he said. "I know you're going through it yourself, you're still grieving, Essence. I will see you in a couple of months."

"Bye, Michael."

I then went to see Lucy and have a catch up. She's all clean now and promised to never have unprotected sex with her punters again and that the guy who gave her the STI, she is actually seeing him, he's got the all clear too.

"I told you, Essence, that I really liked him, that's why I did what I did. I am also thinking about giving up lap dancing, I just want to concentrate on my career. But enough of me, Joyful had a leaving do and it was just a sham, hardly anyone turned up!"

I wasn't surprised at what Lucy was telling me as she deserved it.

"Shame we didn't get to plan it like we said." I laughed.

My dad always taught me to respect my elders but she is beyond vile. She made up so many stories about us all to suit herself, but when we found out she would say it wasn't just her that said it but would never give a name. I am glad she has left, I wouldn't have gone either, it was mainly the bosses there. She received her gold clock and that was that.

"Have you any more gossip?" I asked.

Of course she did. "Well, you're not going to believe this, one off the bosses caught—"

"Who?" I asked impatiently.

"Essence, give me a chance and I will tell you. So as I was saying, one of the bosses caught Kevin snorting drugs. The thing is we all knew in the office but to be caught by the boss. Of course he has been suspended until further notice."

"Oh fuck. I hope he's okay, any more gossip?" I asked.

"Yes, I have loads to share. Angelica the one in the corner over there, you wouldn't believe it, she has started to wear exactly the same clothes as me, shoes and all. I noticed a month ago but it was only small things but now it seems she cloned herself into me. She even dyed her hair. I complained but it was brushed under the carpet."

"And?" I said. "You should be flattered, Lucy. What are you complaining for?"

"I am just worried it's going to get out of hand. Sometimes I clock her looking at me. Such a weird cow, I am sure she's not all there!"

"You're just gonna have to keep an eye out, Lucy, now you have told me I will too!" I laughed.

Chapter *Twenty-three*

I decided to pop round and see Kevin. Some guy opened the door. "Hey, is Kevin in, please?"

"Yes, just a minute while I go get him." He closed the door slightly, "Darling, there is someone at the door for you, hon, can you hear me."

I thought it was a bit strange how he referred to him, sounds like they are partners. Kevin came to the door a bit sheepish.

"Come in Essence."

As we entered the living room the guy who answered the door introduced himself. "Hi, Essence, my name's Joe. I am Kevin's partner."

If the ground could have swallowed Kevin at that very moment it would have. None of us knew he was gay as he slept with a few of the girls at work.

"Hon, I am just going out for a spell Make sure you make Essence a drink. Bye. See you later, nice to meet you, Essence." Joe said as he kissed Kevin on the cheek and left.

Kevin made us a drink and we sat. "Sorry about that," he said.

"I don't understand, is he your partner? If so why are you acting so weird, are you ashamed of him?" I asked.

"No! that's the point, I am ashamed of me."

"For what?" I ask.

He said, "I have always known I was gay and when I told my dad, I was maybe twelve years old, he beat the living shit out of me. *'No son of mine is going to be a gay boy! You fucking disgrace! If I ever hear you mention it again I will kill you.'* My dad was a violent man, he beat my mother almost every day, she was too scared to protect me. After that beating Mum took me to my room, dressed my cuts and badly bruised body and said, 'Son, listen to what he says, and tell no one because he will kill you.' When I turned fourteen I started taking drugs. That bastard's words never left me. I left school. I begged for money to feed my habit. I would lay my head wherever I could sometimes, sleeping in doorways and alleyways. I would go home when I knew he was at work. Mum would let me have a shower and made me a hot meal. She knew I wouldn't come home while he was there so she always made me a pack up for the evening. She was black and blue from all the beatings. I asked her all the time why she didn't leave him. Her answer would always be where would I go?

"He died when I was sixteen. We didn't go to the funeral, just his family attended. It was like a great relief to Mum and me, and the only way Mum could have left him, but he died, and left her. I moved back in, went to college, worked really hard to get my grades so I could do the job I am doing now.

"His words never left my mind, though they were embedded. That's why I continue to take drugs and will not tell anyone I am gay. I am too ashamed and although he is not here he said he would kill me." You see in his eyes that his heart was still broken.

"Kevin, you are about to lose your job. You have to tell your boss everything you have told me and clean up your act. I will come with you if you like. You shouldn't be ashamed of your preference in men. Being gay is not a disease, it's who you are, no one cares nowadays, you do not have to hide away. Take a hold of your life and come out and be proud of yourself and who you are, set yourself free."

"Essence, I am not ready, you're the only one who knows."

"But when you go out where on earth do you go? It must be another planet because you can bet your bottom dollar if it's around here people will know you are gay. In the nicest way possible way, you are nothing special, half the world is gay." I think my words shocked him a little. "I will not bullshit you, Kevin, I know your dad was a bastard to you but why on earth are you making him still rule your life? You have got to move him out of your head, where he still resides. You are his prisoner still after all these years. If you want to break free you really need to find that key. I am always here for you, Kevin, but you seriously have to talk to a professional, someone who can gently move all your thoughts and feelings. No doubt you will always have my ears and I will never lie to you but I cannot free you, and until you are ready to free yourself no one can. I love and will always support you, but you need to see someone. It worked for me so it's worth a shot."

Kevin just looked at me whilst I spoke, my words hitting him. A tear fell from his eye.

"Essence, you are right, I know what you're saying but it's not going to easy thank you for being there for me and understanding. I need to talk to Joe first and tell him truth. He doesn't know that I've kept him quiet for so long, but he deserves to know the truth. I will need him by my side too. I will speak to someone, I can't go on like this forever, I know that. I love you, Es."

"I love you too, Kev. the hardest step is always the one we never want to take but know we have to and like I said, I will always be here for you. No one said it's gonna be easy and things won't change overnight, but eventually everything will be just right, don't rush it, go at your own pace, plus Joe seems lovely and I'm sure he will understand, and he's cute too."

Joe smiled and we hugged for a while, and I stayed for another hour and we just talked, talked about what I had gone through and he told me more about his childhood, it was nice for both of us, a little weight lifted off our shoulders, I know that I'm only just starting to heal and from something completely different to Kevin but sometimes just knowing you have someone there for you makes life seem that easier. I eventually had to make my excuses to leave.

"I have to head off home now but be sure to call me if you should need a word and when you are ready to go see your boss.."

"Of course I will. And, Es, thanks again!"

"See you soon, Kev."

Chapter *Twenty-four*

As I was driving from Kevin's I thought I was being followed but they drove off when they saw that I had clocked them in my rear view mirror, then again I could just be being paranoid

When I got home there was another huge bunch of flowers and they were from Patrick. We have only been on a few dates and I feel suffocated already. I had to ring him. "Hey Patrick, Thank you for the flowers, but you don't have to keep buying things for me. I'm good. I appreciate them but please stop."

"Essence, baby, You're my girl and I want to spoil you."

Baby? His girl? What the fuck? Is this man on crack?

"But, Patrick, we have only been on a few dates, we hardly know each other."

"Well I hope this will turn into a relationship."

"Patrick, I think you should just slow down a bit. If we should get into a relationship we have to be on the same page." I explained.

"Can I see you tonight, Essence?"

"I will let you know, Patrick, I am busy tonight so I will call you tomorrow."

He put the phone down in a bit of huff.

I was in disbelief, he told me at the beginning there was no rush and now he's the one rushing! Was this my fault? Did I ring him too soon? I was asking myself all sorts of questions, but I always came to the conclusion, that he needs to back off.

He must have texted me five or six times after that; I never answered.

Next minute he was at my door.

"Essence, I had to see you! You weren't answering my texts."

"Patrick, I already told you I would call you tomorrow."

"Essence, please just give me an answer!"

"Oh okay! I will see you tomorrow, Patrick, but you really need to go now. My friend will be coming round soon."

"This friend is it a he or a she?" he asked.

How dare he! Who the hell does he think he is?

"No, Patrick! Why should that matter? I have male and female friends. Friends, Patrick! Why are you questioning me? I will see you tomorrow."

He didn't want to leave but I had nothing more to say so closed the door on him. He finally went but he sat in his car for at least half an hour, pretending to be on his phone.

I phoned Lucy to come and keep me company and that's when he left, as he saw a female come round.

Lucy was on her way out with her new beau; she just called to see me free of Patrick, and she left thereafter.

Door locked and chain back on. Text after text from him. Now I am finding his behaviour a bit too much, I just text back saying, 'Goodnight, Patrick' and then turned my phone off. I set my alarm on Dad's radio, thank God I had it. I dread to see how many texts I'm going to have received in the morning.

I was struggling to get to sleep. I swear I could hear a car outside, I peek out the window, and for once I wasn't dreaming, there was a car with the headlights shining into my living room. I scrambled for my phone to call someone, anyone but they drove off.

I slept with one eye open, I even considered ringing Calvin, I was seriously frightened, but then I thought well I have moved to a new area, well back to an old area, I grew up here, but it's so different now, this must be how it is now and Dad just didn't tell me.

I woke up extremely tired this morning but I had no plans for the day so just a quick shower and new PJs on, breakfast on my lap and watching crap TV. I turn my phone on and the amount of texts and a phone calls is ridiculous.

First one I read:

'I am sorry about last night turning up at your door.'

Next: 'Are you going to answer my text?

'Can we go out tomorrow night, Essence?'

'Can you please answer me?'

'I really like you, Essence.'

'For god's sake answer me.'

'Essence? Hello?'

'Why are you ignoring me?'

The texts continue like that. Obviously, I couldn't answer as my phone was off, and when he called all of 24 times, he would have known that.

Now I am sitting here thinking do I call him, but I didn't need to; my phone rang and it was him. "Hi, Patrick."

"Thank goodness," he said sounding really concerned. I thought that was really sweet.

"Of course, Patrick, I am fine, I turned my phone off last night as I needed to rest."

"Did you have a good evening with your friend?"

I stuttered a bit as I knew I was lying, and just said, "Yes, it was fine."

"Can I see you tonight?" he asked.

"Okay! But nothing flash, just a quiet drink would be nice?"

"I will pick you up at seven-thirty."

"Great, I will see you then."

"Have a good day, Patrick."

He was getting too much, but how do you let someone down when they're being nice and trying so hard.

Next thing I know there was a knock at the door; a gift from him. A plain gold chain with two hearts on it. 'Can you wear this tonight?' the note inside read. He had already sent it before he knew I would go out with him. What the fuck? "One more chance Essence just give him one more." I tell myself.

The night was simple, yet lovely. It seems he was genuinely worried about me last night. He really spoils me, with all the flowers and gifts, and as much as I tell him to stop, I do love being treated this way. All this never happened with Calvin, this kind of thing only happens to girls like Aurora. He must like me a lot.

Chapter *Twenty-five*

TWO DAYS LATER

I couldn't sit around all day, having all this time off with next to nothing to do I'm getting bored, so I get dressed and head out to get some paint. I decided I was going to paint the kitchen, start making my new home, mine I couldn't choose the colour so I didn't bother, picking colours and then trying to think of what decor and appliances to have was a nightmare, so just like that I thought fuck it, time for some retail therapy instead. I had my nails done, painted red, they looked lush. I bumped into Mavis in town. She's the one who got me to the top of the list for the job I do, the one that Joyful was talking absolute bollocks to about Lucy. We decided to go for lunch and a catch up.

"How are you?" she asked, but before I could answer she told me how she had lost her mother and that it's the worst pain she had ever felt. She also questioned her own mortality, but she got through it she concentrated on looking after her siblings, plus she had her four children to think about. Instead of looking after herself she thought of all the people around her she turned to drinking wine every night, cooking, obsessed with cleaning, and buying the children whatever they wanted, that's how she showed her love. "I can now see through all the black clouds," she said.

After all that she asked me again how I was and how I was coping. "I will get there, Mavis." I just didn't feel the need to talk about it anymore, that's all I have done, I'm talked out.

"When are you coming back to work? You are so missed!" That was really nice of her to say.

"I will be back in a couple of months as I miss you all too."

We talked some more and put the world to rights, as us women do when we get together, until it was time for us both to make a move.

"See you soon, Mavis."

I gave her a hug and headed home

Unsurprisingly more flowers adorned my doorstep. My house is starting to look like a florist, he must have bought me every colour he could get his hands on and the amount of money he must have spent.

He picked me up on the dot seven-thirty.

"What are we doing tonight, Patrick? As I only want a few drinks, any pub will do."

He didn't say anything he just smiled.

He had other ideas; he took me back to his house. It was absolutely stunning, everything was colour coordinated and in its place. He lead me to his dining room, the table was laid, red roses all the way down. The table seated many people but it was laid just for the two of us, and he pulled out my chair.

"Take a seat, Essence." Before heading to the other side so we were eye to eye, it was like a scene from a Disney princess film, "Would you like some champagne?" he asked.

In my mind I just wanted a normal glass of white wine and soda as I wasn't planning on drinking as my body is still a little too fragile, but he is a doctor so I thought what the hell. "Yes please!"

"I hope you're hungry," he said.

Oysters were our entree, I didn't care for it, the texture in my mouth, eww, but I swallowed it. I didn't want to appear ungrateful. He hired a server for the evening, I felt so special. First course, main and dessert, it was all so luxurious. I was so full I could have burst.

He took me too his living room. I felt like a small fish in an ocean, it was huge. I asked him how long he had lived here.

"Just a few years," he said. "It could be ours."

"What? Don't be silly, Patrick, I have my own home and I am happy there, my Dad gave it to me, it will be my forever home."

"I will move in with you then."

"Stop messing around!"

"Essence, you're my girl now."

I was taken aback because he meant every word. To be honest he was freaking me out. I knew right at that moment that he wasn't the one for me. I didn't know how I was going to excuse myself, so I ask to go to bathroom. He actually took me right to the door. Whilst I was in the bathroom I had a word with myself; "Essence, you are strong, you can do this, tell him you have to go." He was still at the door waiting for me. As we got downstairs I said to him, "Patrick, I need to go home, the oysters have made me feel nauseous."

"Your bed is made up for you," he said.

"No, Patrick! I want to go home!"

He was hesitant but he finally agreed to take me home.

They drive back was the longest drive of my life, it was silent and awkward, and I couldn't wait to be out of this man's company.

We finally pulled up and I jumped out of the car I didn't wait for him to open the door.

As I walked to my front door I heard Patrick walking behind me.

"Can I come in with you?" he asked.

"Are you fucking serious?" I said in my head, but to him I was obviously more polite, "No, Patrick, I need to be by myself."

"Please, just let me look after you?"

"No, Patrick, I will be fine!"

He tried to give me a kiss but I jolted back.

"Can I not kiss you now?" he said.

"Not unless you want me to throw up on you!"

He walked off like a mardy child and got back in his car. I locked and chained the door behind me. I peeked through my window; he was still there. He texted me: 'Are you in bed yet?'

'No, I am going up now, Patrick.'

I quickly ran upstairs and turned my bedroom light on, gave myself five minutes before I turn the lights off. I could hear his car revving up to leave. He then drove away.

I was so on edge after the events of the evening, and the first person I thought to call was Calvin so that's exactly what I did. He was surprised to hear from me. I could hear that bitch Jane in the background.

"Who's that? and why are they calling at this time of the night? Who is it Cal?"

Calvin just told her to shut the fuck up, he never said it was me on the other end. "What's up?" he asked,

"Calvin can you please come stay with me tonight?"

"On my way," he said, not one bit of hesitation, he didn't even ask me why.

"I'm not at the apartment, I'm at my Dad's, do you remember the address?"

"Yeah, yeah, of course I do. Be there soon."

Within twenty minutes he was here. "What's going on?" he asked?

I told him everything.

"You don't make things easy do ya?" he chuckled.

"What I didn't mean for any of this to happen! A toxic doctor was the last thing on my dating list." We laughed together, it felt natural, it was nice to see him.

"I will stay with you as long as you need me."

"Thank you, Calvin, but it's just for tonight, you can stay in the spare room, and it's all made up."

Through the night I heard a car pull up, headlights shining in my living room, the same as before. I called Calvin, who went to investigate and they drove off.

"Calvin, can you stay in my room? But don't get any ideas. Nothing is going to happen, I'm not leading you on, I just wanted to feel safe and you were the first person that came to mind. We are just friends, okay?!"

"Okay Essence," he replied and again with no hesitation, he got straight into bed.

Through the night we were spooning just as we did when we were together but that's as far as it went. I felt no attraction too him anymore but I was so grateful he dropped everything for me. I slept okay that night as I knew he was there to protect me.

The next day I was bombarded with text messages. 'Who was that guy at our house?' Patrick asked.

'Patrick, it's not our house, it's my house!'

'You said you weren't feeling well, Essence, that's why you went home, you lied to me!'

I decided to call him, I didn't want to hide behind a text.

"Patrick, I can't see you anymore," Everything is happening too quickly and I don't want a relationship with you or anyone, I'm not ready."

He was furious. "So I spent all that money on you for nothing?"

"I didn't ask you to, Patrick! You can have your necklace back and some of the flowers are still alive."

"Don't be so sarcastic!" he said,

"I really wasn't!" I stuttered. "Anyway, Patrick, I'm hanging up now."

All I could hear before I hung up was, "You can't hang up on me."

I turned my phone on silent. God, I wish my Dad was here, he would know what to do.

Calvin eventually got up. I made him some breakfast and before he left he said, "Call me at any time if you need me, I will get here as quick as I can."

I was truly grateful although I didn't tell him that. I just said, "Thank you. And, Calvin, don't forget what I said last night."

He then let himself out. "Essence!" he shouted as he was leaving. "There's a big bunch of white lilies on your doorstep."

For fucks sake, Patrick doesn't mess around, I had only got off the phone to him a couple of hours ago, I went to get them. On the card it said, 'Rest in peace'. Something told me to keep the card but of course I threw the flowers in the bin, at that moment I didn't feel scared as I had Calvin here, he decided to stay with for a little longer, "Es, I'm going to go ring Jane and let her know something came up so I won't be home just yet, I'm not leaving you right now. Just in case."

"Thanks, that means a lot."

Calvin went to his car to call Jane

I sat in my Dad's chair, just thinking about everything that has gone on between Patrick and me, I am so glad I ended whatever it was that was going on between us before anything serious started. With everything that has happened lately it wasn't the right time for me. He did take my mind off things though, but I really didn't want or need to get in a relationship and I am sure I told him that. Did I lead him on? I did want him to kiss me. Well, I think I did, but I never ever stated I wanted a relationship. I could never imagine he would be this way, he is a doctor for God's sake.

Chapter *Twenty-six*

THE WEEK AFTER THE ONE BEFORE

The phone calls and the texts continued, I didn't answer the calls but I did read the texts. Some were normal but others were downright vile with what he wanted to do to me. He would switch constantly; he went from loving me and calling me his 'girl' to he wanted me dead – 'If I can't have you no one else can' and 'I will make you look so ugly, no one will look you.

I had to answer those texts. I asked him, 'What do you mean? Are you threatening me? I will call the police, Patrick!'

'Sorry! My phone has been hacked.' The lying bastard, he's realised he's fucked up sending me everything on text. I know damn well it's him.

'You aren't fooling anyone, Patrick!' I replied. 'Leave me alone!'

Am I stupid? I work for a law firm.

I call Michael and tell him about it all. He said exactly what I thought, keep all the texts, the cards, everything. "I will get a restraining order signed by the judge sent to him as soon as possible, don't worry, Essence."

I felt somewhat relieved but still extremely on edge.

After a couple of days he received the restraining order, and straight off the bat he texted saying, 'You bitch! One way or the other!' and that was it. What the hell did he mean? "Oh well fuck it, he couldn't do anything, I don't care what he's saying because he can't come near me." I thought and blocked his number.

I want to go out and get a little merry and forget about Doctor Patrick, the prick, but I know I can't as my liver still needs to heal so I will head to the gym instead, anything to distract me.

I go out my front door and on the drive were black petals and a small wooden box. I rang the police. They say there is nothing they can do as I couldn't prove it was with him. I decided there and then to get cameras all around my house. I won't and can't let that bastard scare me any longer. I put my big girl pants on and leave to go the gym just as I said I was going too. I decided to walk as well as I won't let any man make me feel intimidated.

As I was walking to the gym my thoughts ran across to the man with no name. I couldn't have got into a relationship with Doctor Patrick as I knew he was the only one for me, even though Patrick distracted me for a moment with his fake persona. How do I get him to notice me? I know he has noticed me but not for the right reason, I fainted in his arms for goodness sake and before that I once uttered "Hello" whilst looking like a sweaty mess, but I want him to notice me as myself, so next time I see him I will make sure he does notice me. I still don't want a relationship mind, but to get close to the man constantly in my dreams would be just *sigh*, but I am a strong woman and who says a woman can't make the first move?

I arrive at the gym, I work my arse off. With the stone that I have already lost I feel great and it's like I already have a head start. I step on the scales to see if there is any change and surprisingly I have now lost a stone and a half, thanks to Patrick for the stress, I guess.

Straight after I do my session, God it felt good! I go shopping for some new gym attire. I pick the sexiest I can lay my hands on, and I am now in a size medium, plus some new trainers too.

My dad left me a lot of money so I say thank you to him for these. I know he is with me, cheering me on. Every time I think of him it really hurts my heart, that he is no longer here.

I crave an alcoholic beverage as that's the only thing that gives me solace so I head to the wine bar. I buy myself a bottle of champagne,

"let's go for the good stuff but not too ridiculously pricey" I tell the bartender, I've got a lot of money but not that much, he hands me a bottle of *Veuve Clicquot*, it's my new fave. I pick up the phone to call Aurora. She joins me within half an hour, dressed quite casually, no makeup on either, which I am glad about as I am still in my gym wear and laden with shopping bags, and I am still smarting with her.

We get to talking and I have to ask her why she thinks it's acceptable for her to leave me on night outs we arrange for some bloke. She simply didn't understand what I was talking about, so I explained to her like a five year old, and I think she finally understood.

She is now saying her sugar daddy hasn't turned out to be who she thought he was. He brought her all her clothes, shoes and bags, she wasn't allowed to choose anything herself he was trying to clone her into his late wife who was as old as he was, and now she doesn't know how to get out of it. They have a routine and have eat at the same time, morning, noon and night; she has to wear the same kind of night gown as his wife did and spray herself in the same perfume But even after all of that what made Aurora open her eyes was that she had to wear his late wife's jewellery.

I had little to no sympathy for her; she chose him for his green over our friendship – what am I meant to say to her? I pretend to listen but realistically, I don't give a shit. She made her bed. I love her so much, and I would never put a man above her as when you build up a friendship like ours from school, nothing or no one should get in between. She is like the sister I never had and I will always protect her no matter what or who comes into our lives and I can't and still don't understand why she doesn't see it like that.

She wants my advice on how to let him down gently but feels that she can't do it at the same time. I've heard enough so I just said to her, "Tell him point blank that you don't appreciate being told how to act or dress and that it's time for you to move on."

Neither of us are having any luck with men at the moment. She suggests we go on holiday but right now I want to concentrate on myself so I decline,

"Don't be so boring!" she says.

That got my back up straight away. I told her I wasn't going to be her back up plan ever again. She began arguing with me. I just got up and walked out with the words, "When you grow up call me!"

As I got home with the remainder of my champagne I suddenly feel so horny. I haven't had real sex for quite a while and the last time I did was with Calvin. The earth didn't quiver. So it's me and my rampant rabbit. I will need to dust it off though and maybe find some batteries, as I haven't used it for a long while. Now where is it?

It's still in its box under the bed with my private things, letters etcetera. I glimpse another box next to it.

I opened it, it was full of letters my Dad had got from my mother. They were all dated as well, so he didn't send all her mail back then. They were all addressed to me. At the moment I can't even consider opening them as she has no relevance in my life. I can't forgive her for leaving my Dad and me. I have truly never felt hate for someone ever in my life but its close with her.

The horniness has gone now, it is replaced with *Shall I or shall I not read these letters?* I decide not to as like I said earlier, I can't forgive her. I put some music on hoping it will ease my mind. Who am I kidding? Everything that's been going on in my life lately you couldn't make it up. All I want is to live without any sorrow, any drama, anything negative.

In reality everyone is going through some kind of shit in their lives, and they seem to get on with it, why can't I? For me, it seems never ending. Losing a big part of your life is mega, it's so raw at the moment as it hasn't been long. I want to call my dad, I want to talk to him. He would make every problem seem so silly and tell me it's not worth my tears or anger. How I am going to live without him? His wise words? His cuddles? Him just not being? I will never see him again. I can't even comprehend how much this has impacted on my life and then to see all the letters from that bitch, it beggars belief, she didn't want me. I decide after an hour to take a look in the box, it was calling me to do so. I open the box and put them all in order. There was so many of them, the first one was when I was six, so for a year and a bit I was an afterthought.

I open the letter. *To my beautiful girl*. I start welling up, "For fucks sake Essence, get it together," I tell myself, I compose myself and carry on.

To my beautiful girl,

Do not ever think that I left you because of you. I love you so much but I had to leave because I just didn't love Daddy anymore. I wanted to take you with me but there was nowhere for you to stay. My heart simply broke the day I left you behind, you probably cannot remember me leaving and you won't have seen my tears, but I cried so much. I almost changed my mind but I knew couldn't stay, I just wasn't in love with your Dad. I loved him but not enough to stay, I am so sorry, Essence, all my love always, Mummy, please forgive me. xx

I cannot believe she has said I probably couldn't remember that day, I will never forget that day. I cried for her so much. I hoped she would come back for me but she never did, she didn't come back. Seeing this letter has made me feel dismayed and confused and to be honest I am really pissed with her words, written to me at such a young age. This is probably why my Dad shielded me from them, as he knew it would upset me. I don't think I will read another one so back in the box they go. My so called mother is the last person I need on my mind right now.

Eight-fifteen p.m., I am going to bed with my half bottle of champagne. I put my favourite music on, Whitney Houston, no one can touch that beautiful voice. I feel myself falling asleep, again I'm dreaming of the man with no name. I must find out his full name as I hope to have his surname one day, he is the only one for me. At this moment it's only a fantasy but I will ride with it until it comes true.

Wait.

What if he has a girlfriend? Or a wife? I didn't even contemplate any of this, as he is always on his own when I have bumped into him at the gym or anywhere else.

I can't believe I never thought about that before, how self-centred am I?

Just because I was now single and out of my dull, boring relationship with the even more dull Calvin, for me to assume that he was also single because I am. Ha-ha what a dick. I do need to find that out though, I need to know if he could be mine, he's perfect, and sexy, and handsome and everything that is nice, and I can't get him out of my head.

Chapter *Twenty-seven*

A couple of months ago I told myself I needed to concentrate and knuckle down and get my life in order and I wrote a list of to-dos, all of which were easily achievable and I promised myself I would stick to the plan. And now those two months have passed and I haven't stuck to anything on that list, for example, stop drinking alcohol: I have cut down but I haven't stopped, here I am now filling my glass with gin and tonic. To be fair I have got a lot more tonic than my normal half each measure.

I did however stick with the gym though, and of course I keep seeing the man with no name but I feel like he never sees me. My body is getting really toned now and I'm feeling a better within myself, I feel like I can face the world, in a bikini, ha-ha. And on another note I haven't seen or heard from Patrick in like a six or seven weeks either.

I'm back at work now too, nothing has changed much there. Lucy made sure she filled me in on some of the gossip. I couldn't wait to hear more but I have to get on with my work too, my workload is mega at the moment, it's like no one did anything whilst I was off, like no one thought, 'Oh, Essence is off, she's having a rough time and she probably has deadlines, let's help her out.'

Michael is such a mess, he looks unkempt, he hasn't shaved in what looks like months, his suits and shirts are always creased. I don't think he has showered either, his body odour is bad, like really bad, it's oozing from him, but mostly you can see he's so unhappy and I do feel for him but all he is going through he created. I'm thinking of ways to tell him about his BO though at the moment, because it's offending quite a few of us in the office, but how do you tell someone that they stink let alone your boss? I'm sure I will find a way. Lucy was telling me that Michael's wife has left him, and that she has kicked him out, and he has no alternative but to go to his mistress as he has nowhere else to go, he has been so miserable. He puts on a smile and pretends he is happy as Amanda is about to have their child, but he isn't fooling anyone.

I went to his office to see him.

"Essence, come in, take a seat." He said with a smile that was obviously forced, his office smelt worse than he did.

"Michael, please tell me if I'm intruding but I couldn't help but notice that you really aren't yourself, you look terrible, and you don't smell too good either but just like you said to me before I'm here if you need to talk."

Well he didn't need any more than that, he broke down and told me so much, he said that he already has grown up children who have left home, he could have never imagined he would have another baby. He was beside himself, he desperately wants his wife to take him back.. He works all day and drinks all night. He doesn't and never did love Amanda, she was just an easy lay. The more he gave her, gifts, clothes, jewellery, the more sex she would give him.

Amanda didn't realise he was only using her, that's why she came off the pill, thinking that he truly loved her as he had said it many times whilst they were in bed together. He showered her with so much bullshit talking about 'love', she actually believed it. The gifts he gave her sealed the deal, so she thought. He even gave her a promise ring, thinking he could dump her at any time.

Never in his wildest dreams did he think she would get pregnant and when his wife found out about Amanda he was shocked and knew he was fucked. He slept with other women and got away with it. This time he took on a fiery woman. Amanda didn't give a second thought about his wife, Michael was now hers and hers alone, she was beyond happy.

Michael's only escape was work; he stayed later and later. He didn't want to be at Amanda's house, it wasn't and never would be his home. He truly wanted to go to his wife; that was his home. He rang her constantly, she just never answered.

Our conversation was interrupted, the office phone rang, someone on the other side of the room picked up.

"Essence? Phone, it's for you!" they shouted, I apologised to Michael and went back to my desk.

"Okay, put them through to me. Who is it?"

"Some man, I think he said his name was Calvin?"

What the fuck is he calling me for? And at work, for fuck's sake. "Oh okay, yeah thanks, pop him through."

"Calvin? What can I do for you? I haven't heard from you in weeks."

"Can you please come around and see me later, Essence?"

"What for?" I asked?

"Please, Es, I need to talk to you."

"Calvin, what could you possibly have to talk to me about?"

"I will tell you! I promise, I just need to talk to you, can you come round tonight?"

"No, I am busy, give me a couple of days and I will call you, I can't just drop everything."

"I understand, I know I hurt you."

"Don't flatter yourself, I didn't think of you for too long, I will call you!"

To be truthful I wanted to hear what he had to say now, and I wanted to go straight to him but I don't want to him to think I will come running as soon as asks. I Know he came to me when I needed him before with Patrick but this is different, he didn't say he was in trouble and to be fair after he stayed with me that night, I haven't seen or heard from him until now, it was like he fell off the face of the earth so he can wait.

I kept myself busy for a few days, work, gym, and God I hit that gym hard. I was also decorating my home; there was still a few mores changes I needed to make but its finally falling into place.

I couldn't wait any longer, I gave in and phoned him.

It was a three and a half days.

"Hi, Calvin, it's me, I can meet you tonight at the pub on the corner where we always used to go."

"No, Essence, can you come around to my house?"

"Not on your nelly," I said. "It's the pub or nothing."

"Ok, okay!" he said. "I will meet you at eight."

Me being my stubborn self said, "No I will meet you at half seven."

"Okay, thank you, Es, see you then."

I was wondering what the hell he wanted to speak to me about.

The time soon came around but I decided I would turn up for eight; I owe him nothing. Even though he was there for me like I said before, I still needed to make sure he knew what he had done wasn't okay, and I wouldn't be treated that way and then fall at his feet when he wanted to. Makes me sound like a petty bitch but he does deserve it.

I got to the pub and he was sitting in our spot where we always sat. My drink was already on the table, rum and black. "Sorry I am late, I was watching TV and the time just ran away with me." Of course I wasn't, I just left him hanging for a while.

"Drink that!" he said. "I will get us another." He, got up and went to the bar, as he came back to the table. I noticed his hands were shaking,

"Why are you shaking?" I asked. "Are you okay?"

"Yes, I am just nervous."

I looked him straight in his eyes. About what?" I asked.

"First of all, Es, you look beautiful, have you lost some weight? You look and smell so good, can I give you a cuddle?"

"If you put your hands on me, Calvin, I will walk out of here quicker than I came in. You asked me here for a reason, what is it?"

"Es, I have made the biggest mistake of my life. I miss you and to me you will always be the one. I'm so sorry. Please take me back!"

"Are you absolutely fucking kidding me, Calvin? What the fuck has that got to do with me? You made that choice, you cheated on me and more than once."

"Essy, listen to me!" he said.

"What Calvin?"

"I really want you back, I am so sorry for what I said and for what I did to you, please give me another chance, I can make it up to you, I promise, I swear to you I'll do whatever it takes, I will give you a few days to think about it!"

I cannot believe he has the audacity to even ask me this and then tell me he will give me few days to think, I sat back in my chair and take a sip of my rum and black. His eyes haven't left me.

"Calvin, if you were the last man on this earth, I wouldn't take you back. You are the most boring, dull and... well I used to think that but clearly I was wrong, you saved the exciting, 'attractive' side of you for all the slags you chose over me! I honestly don't know why I stayed with you for as long I did. You did me a favour leaving me!" I was seething but I knew I needed to calm down. I watched him as he watched me, waiting for what I was going to say next.

I calmed down, I supposed he deserved that.

", I can't lie, I will be forever grateful to you Calvin. You saved my life, and you were there for me straight away and without hesitation when I had issues with Patrick and I told you that night that I didn't want to give you the wrong impression and that we are only friends. I feel nothing for you like that now, Calvin, you are with Jane, you're going to be a daddy!"

"Essy. Please—"

"No, Calvin, just stop! You don't need to go any further, the answer is no, never. I wish you all the best, in all you do. Take care of you, Calvin. Bye."

I got up from my chair and walked away, not even a glace back.

That part of my life, is over.

As I was walking away I thought what a fucking cheek, as if I would go back with him, my life has been turned upside down this year, I have been through so much and from this moment I will only do what's best for me.

I soon arrive home. I took a breath and then a another. I felt a sigh of relief. Calvin left a few messages on my phone, I didn't even listen to them. I just deleted them.

I can't wait until tomorrow night. Lucy and I are going out to this new nightclub, Honey Bees, and no casual clothes are permitted, so I'm dressing to impress and I'm really going to let my hair down and have an amazing time with my best friend.

So it's early night for me, lock and chain the door behind me as always and straight to bed.

Chapter *Twenty-eight*

The morning seems to come around quickly, I'm not at work today either, so I'm having a nice filling breakfast, bacon, eggs, two slices of toast and a cuppa.

After breakfast I go to my favourite place, my closet ha-ha. What am I going to wear tonight? Something tight and flattering, I find the perfect outfit, it is just stunning, my toned body held it like a glove. I got my stilettos out and bag too. Now what to do today? I cleaned the house from top to bottom. Then I thought, fuck it, I'm going to start getting ready for tonight, nice and chilled, first to paint my nails, toes and all. I cleanse my face then leave it to breathe before I apply my make up later. I have a long, hot shower, washing my hair. I think of the man with no name; he raises something in me like no other. Shampoo burning my eyes, I didn't even flinch, I was masturbating. I seem to be doing this a lot just lately. What? I'm on my own now.

I get out of the shower, steam coming from my body. I drape my towel around me like I was the softest petal in the garden. I didn't dry myself properly, the towel drops to the floor and I apply my baby oil, slip into my satin dressing gown and start to dry my hair. The heat of the hair dryer makes me feel flushed. I put in my clip-in hair extensions and straighten my hair so it reaches to the middle of my back. Now to apply my make up, it takes me almost an hour as I wanted to look as amazing as I felt. I took so much time that it seems to have ran away from me today. Lucy would be here in half an hour. I get into my back skimming dress, no bra for me tonight, actually no underwear at all. I step into my shoes, sweep on another coat of red lipstick.

Lucy arrived. "Wow!" she said to me. "You look amazing!"

As we arrived at the club, cocktails it is. I glance around the room and who should I clock? The man with no name. And he was looking at me too. I blushed and looked away. The music was so loud, Lucy and I couldn't hear each other speak so I shouted, "Let's go dance!"

"Let's get another drink first!" was her reply.

I looked over to where he was before and he was still there looking right at me. I drank that cocktail so quickly as I was shaking on the inside.

"He's looking at me," I said to Lucy.

"Who?"

"My dream guy, from the gym, the one with no name!"

"Maybe this is your night!" she shouted in my ear.

We made our way to dance floor. Lucy happened bumped into some of the girls from her other job so she got dancing and talking with them.

The man with no name came over to me. "Hello," he said.

I almost dropped my drink. "Hello!" I said.

From that moment we flirted throughout the night. My heart was beating so fast I swear I could hear it over the music. A slow song came on and we slow danced. We seemed to talk so intensely, then he kissed me so softly, then it became so intimate. His tongue swivelled mine like a serpent snake and then he pulled me in closer. I could feel every inch of his penis against me. It was so much bigger than I had imagined. I wondered if this was the night I had always dreamt off.

Lucy came over at some point and said that the other girls had invited us to go to another club, and that she really wanted to go.

"You go Luc, I'm fine here." I replied as I looked over at him.

"Enjoy!" Lucy said with a wink, she gave me a kiss on the cheek, "Text me when you get home. Love you Es."

"Will do, love you too!" And they left.

Me and the man with no name had another drink before we too decided it was time to go.

As we left the club we got into a taxi, and I said my address. I wanted no more than him to enter me that night, and we continued to kiss passionately in the back seat of that taxi. As we reached my house he said, "I will take care of the fare."

"Thank you and thank you for a fabulous night," was all I could say.

"Let me walk you to your door?"

We got to my front door and he gave me another kiss and started walking to the taxi, I shouted, "I didn't take your name!"

His response was, "I didn't give it." with a smile, and that was that.

I locked and chained the door behind me. As soon as I got in my rabbit came out. I had to finish what he had started. It didn't take long because I was right there when his penis had rubbed against me so hard. After I pleasured myself I danced around my bedroom. I just didn't want the night to end; I was on cloud nine, ten and eleven. My unspoken love.